Aberaeron, Cardigan

NESTLING in its picturesque harbour, Aberaeron in Wales makes the perfect picture-postcard seaside town. Brightly-painted houses overlook fishing boats in the natural bay — a wonderful scene at twilight under a deep blue sky.

The residents of this sleepy beauty spot are welcoming and charming, rightfully proud of their delightful home and its attractions.

The sea life centre, which rather aptly started life behind the local fish shop, is one of the town's highlights and is well worth a visit.

People's Friend

Contents

p69

❋ ❋ ❋ ❋ ❋ ❋

Dear Reader,

A WARM welcome to the "Friend" Annual for 20●
Inside we've mixed all the right ingredien●
for a great read — romance, humour, nostalgi●
— with 26 brand new Stories, written by your
favourite "Friend" authors, which will warm yo●
heart.

Come rain or shine, Brenda G. Macrow's lovely
poetry will take you through the changing
seasons. There are also great views from arou●
Britain by our cover artist, J. Campbell Kerr.

And you can enjoy a star-studded tour with ●
series of features all about Scotland's most
famous and well-loved films.

So, spare a few moments out of your day to ●
down, relax and enjoy good reading with your
favourite "Friend"!

Your Editor

p74

nual 2003

The Four Seasons
Poetry by
Brenda G. Macrow

p142

Campbell Kerr Paintings

36

On The Silver Screen

Scotland's classic films

p92

p152

5

by Sylvia Wynne

It's The Thou

Illustration by
Richard Eraut.

DID you have a nice Christmas, children?"
Tina Spender asked her class on the first
day back at school after the holiday.
"Yes, miss," the eight year olds chorused.

"And did Father Christmas bring you everything
you wanted?" Tina continued.

At twenty-two, she wasn't altogether sure just what

t That Counts

The People's Friend Annual

eight year olds liked these days — designer trainers, mobile phones, computer games . . .? And she wanted to get it right. In your first year out of college, a class of energetic youngsters could be pretty alarming if you didn't show them who was boss!

"So, today," Tina said firmly, quietening their noisy chatter, "we're going to write thank you letters. I hope you've already written your actual letters for all the nice gifts you received. This is just to show me how good you are at it."

After a few initial groans and protests, Tina finally persuaded the children to settle down to the exercise, writing to "pretend" grans and aunties.

While the children talked quietly, Tina moved to the radiator, and drew her cardigan more tightly around her shoulders against the chilly January morning. As she gazed out of the window, she began thinking about her own unwritten thank you letters.

Robin had sent her a fabulous bracelet. He was working now in a prestigious city firm and earned a good salary.

They'd met at college. Tina, a shy first-year, had been flattered by the attentions of this handsome third-year with the challenging blue eyes.

She sighed, remembering how she'd revelled in his company — until she'd discovered the casual playboy behind the charm. It was then she'd decided Robin was definitely not for her.

An over-indulged only son, he couldn't stick at anything — let alone commit to just one person.

The bracelet was lovely and she'd have to write and thank him for it. She would have sent it back, but that seemed a little cruel.

Adrian had come along next. He was completely different from Robin, and very serious. They had long, intense conversations lasting till dawn. Tina even believed herself to be in love. But, in the end, she realised it was too much too soon. She just wasn't ready for a serious relationship.

Of course, Adrian was upset when she'd ended things. But Tina knew in her heart he'd get over it.

In the end, his career would take over — he was already well established in a publishing firm.

He'd sent her a selection of rather serious novels which she knew, with a sinking heart, she'd never read. Writing her enthusiastic thanks was going to be a problem.

Some of her class had finished their letters and started to chatter. Tina turned back to them with relief. She wouldn't have to think about Tiz and the present he hadn't sent her . . .

John Tizzard. The one man with whom she'd gladly spend the rest of her life — but would most likely never see again.

What was it about John? He wasn't her usual type at all yet, when he smiled at her with a lop-sided quirkiness that was all his own, her heart stood still.

8

It had been love at first sight. They'd been inseparable. John was funny, clever and serious by turns, and Tina felt at ease with him.

She couldn't bear the thought of college ending, and not being able to spend all her spare time with Tiz.

But his heart was set on being a journalist and, after college, he'd left for the city to find himself a job.

He wrote funny, loving letters that couldn't disguise, after his successes at college, his struggle to find work in a competitive field.

Then the letters had stopped.

Weeks later, just before Christmas, Tina ran into him in the high street of their home town.

"*Tiz!* I didn't know you were back!" she'd said, amazed at seeing him again.

"Just dropped in for Christmas. Mum insisted — she wants to feed me up." His tone was light, but Tina could see he hadn't been taking proper care of himself.

"I'm teaching now," she told him. "I wrote and told you."

"Good for you!" John smiled. "You'd be good at that — the sympathetic type."

Tina frowned. There was an anger in his voice which she didn't like. What had happened to her easy-going, happy-go-lucky friend?

"Well — see you!" John turned away. "Don't buy me a Christmas present!"

"Why not?" She couldn't keep the hurt from her voice.

"Oh, just because . . ." John shrugged then turned and was lost among the crowds of Christmas shoppers.

After a couple of days, Tina plucked up the courage to ring him, but was told he was out. Nor did he ring back.

Finally, his mother told her — and she suspected untruthfully — that he'd gone back to London.

TINA collected the class's more or less comprehensible thank-you letters, and sent the children off for their mid-morning break. She loved teaching, she thought, as she busied herself with preparing the next lesson. But she couldn't get over the feeling that there was something missing in her life.

Of course, she had plenty of friends, and her family were delighted she'd found a job so near home. But they were always on the look-out for any signs of a romance!

But none of the men she met held a candle to Tiz.

On her way home, Tina called in at a small newsagent's, determined to buy some writing paper and envelopes and finally get down to her long-neglected thank-you letters.

The dim little shop was empty, apart from the man behind the counter.

She picked up a pad of paper, envelopes and a couple of ball-point pens, and went up to the counter to pay.

"You!" Tina could hardly believe her eyes — it was John Tizzard.

He had smartened up from when she'd seen him before Christmas, and put on a bit of weight at last — his mother's cooking? His gaze met hers.

"That'll cost you . . ." he began

"Are you working here?" she asked.

"I certainly am. The first step in my career — at least it's a paper shop." His tone was defensive.

"And you're living at home?" Tina asked.

"That's right," he said, handing over her change. "I had enough of the big city, or it had enough of me. Unfriendly place."

"I — I'm going to start on my thank-you letters," Tina faltered, playing for time.

He was home. And he hadn't told her . . .

"At least you won't have to do one for me." His tone was cold again, and it chilled her heart to hear it.

"No, that's one less, isn't it? You said not to give you a present," she retorted. "I guess you're not much of a one for Christmas."

"What's in it for me?" he asked bitterly. "What I want can't be bought."

Willie Shand.

Someone came into the shop then, and John moved away to serve them. Tina waited, tapping her foot.

"What's wrong?" she demanded when the customer left. "So you're not an instant success? It takes time, John!"

"But you don't have to take it out on me!" she continued. "I'm the one who believes in you! Your writing's good. Sooner or later you'll make it, even if you have to start off selling in a shop. At least it's a job."

Tina could feel herself going scarlet as they glared at one another.

"Yes, Tina, it's a job, and I'm lucky to have it," he said at last. "At least I can get some writing done in the evenings.

"I'm glad you've got one, too," he added remorsefully. "At least one of us is a success. And, like I said, you'll be a good teacher. Your kids are lucky."

Tina was about to leave when John pulled a small battered package out of his pocket and thrust it into her hand.

Winter Miracle

SKELETAL tree in a desolate landscape
Trapped by the frost in the still of the night,
Stripped of her leaves by the chill winds of autumn,
Lonely she stands amid acres of white.

Only the stars saw the silent encounter,
Saw her transfixed by a glacial breath;
Dawn wrapped its mists like a mantle around her,
Light gave the lie to her semblance of death.

Glittering now like a fabulous jewel,
Gladly she welcomes the sun's warming gold —
Eloquent symbol of Beauty's renewal
After the darkness, the fear and the cold . . .

— *Brenda G. Macrow.*

Near St Andrews.

"Here. I did buy you a present after all, when I got this job," he muttered. "But I was too ashamed to give it to you, considering all the other fancy things you'd be getting —

"Don't open it now, wait till you get home."

SAFE in her room, Tina tore open the paper, only to reveal yet more packaging. Finally, she found a little square box.

Inside was a ring — an eternity ring, studded with tiny turquoise-coloured stones.

Wrapped around it was a piece of paper covered with John's familiar scrawl.

Darling Tina, I wish I could buy you diamonds but, in the meantime, this will have to do. I was too ashamed to give it to you at Christmas. Have it with my love. Always, John.

Tina burst into a flood of tears, holding the little box to her heart. John did care for her, after all!

Then, laying the box carefully down, Tina reached for paper and pen.

Darling Tiz, she wrote, *it's perfect — just what I always wanted! When can we meet? Yours for ever, Tina.*

This was one thank you letter that wrote itself! ❏

A Country

ANDY SHANNON whistled cheerfully as he rode his Starley's Rover bicycle along the sun-dappled country lane, weaving daringly from one side to another as he relished the freedom of a road empty of other traffic.

He rounded the bend and almost cannoned into another cyclist coming towards him.

Braking sharply, they both slewed to a stop, and Andy found himself looking into a pair of startled grey eyes that were growing stormier by the second.

"Hey!" the girl said. "Why don't you look where you're going? You nearly sent me into the ditch!"

She was young, and pretty in a fine-complexioned, snub-nosed sort of way. Coppery curls frizzed out from beneath the beribboned hat which crowned the tailored blue cycling skirt and white blouse that decked her slender form.

Clumsily polite, Andy pulled off his cloth cap and mumbled an apology.

"Sorry, miss. Didn't expect anyone at this time of day. You're another early bird, eh?"

She looked him up and down, her expression saying clearly what she thought of his shabby plus-fours of thick wool, far too hot for the season, and threadbare tweed jacket. All at once the cycling outfit which he had thought so smart was reduced to what it actually was — a well-worn second-hand buy picked up on the market for mere pennies.

"I always take the air before breakfast," she replied grandly. "Cycling is such fine exercise, don't you agree?"

"Aye. And you can cover a fair distance on a bicycle, too. See you've got a Rover, same as mine."

"That's right," she agreed, unbending slightly. "Though yours is in better order, I would think."

It was true. Having saved long and hard for his bicycle, Andy kept the metalwork and leather saddle brightly polished and always dried it off after being out in the rain.

Straightening her handlebars, the girl groped for the pedal with a neatly booted foot, nodded coolly to Andy and pushed off on her way. He watched her cycle off down the sunny lane, the blue ribbons on her hat streaming out behind her. She was like no girl he had ever met before. None of the girlfriends his sisters brought home were in the same league.

And he had let her go and not even asked her name.

d At Heart

Ruefully, Andy headed off to try and find Whittaker's Farm. His mother had been poorly all winter and the doctor said she needed building up with a better diet. The fresh milk and eggs he recommended were not often seen on the table at 76 Finch Street, especially since Andy's father had died.

Andy wished his job at the mill brought in a bit more money. But then a mate had mentioned the farm in the fold of the fells that sold its produce cheaper than anywhere else. It was a long way, but worth it if it meant that Mam was getting the nourishment she needed.

He found the place, made his purchases, together with a wedge of yellow cheese, and counted out his pennies into the farmer's wife's work-reddened palm.

**by
Pamela
Kavanagh**

Illustration by Mark Viney.

"Come up from Burnley, have you, lad?" Mrs Whittaker asked. "That's an uphill ride!"

"It was. Still, it'll be an easier journey back."

"Just watch those eggs, they'll be scrambled, else. Here, let me pack them in a bit of straw."

Andy wanted to enquire if she knew the girl he had met, but an odd shyness prevented him. All the way back to the town, with the basket on his bicycle filled with good things to eat, a pair of stormy grey eyes beneath a fall of coppery curls haunted him.

Next Sunday, he planned, he would bring a bite to eat and spend the whole day on the fell. He was sure to see her, and he could always call at the farm for the food on the way back.

"Proper milk!" his mother exclaimed with a smile. "Better than the watered-down stuff we buy off the cart. Brown eggs, too. Real farm butter *and* cheese. My, aren't I spoiled!"

Mam had been brought up on a farm and knew first-class produce when she saw it.

"You must eat it yourself," Andy said. "No giving it all to our Rose and Daisy." His sisters were both working, and Mam insisted they, too, needed feeding up.

THE heatwave continued, and the following Sunday was hotter than ever. Andy abandoned the heavy plus fours for lightweight, well-worn but neatly laundered trousers and shirt, asked his mother to prepare him some bread and cheese, and set off. But, though he was careful to take the same route at exactly the same time, the girl was not there.

Andy cycled on to the village of Ridgebeck and rested a while on the green under a shady tree, watching the congregation leave the church. She wasn't amongst those either. He lingered there, hoping she would appear, while the sun climbed higher in the sky and the day grew hotter.

In the end, Andy mounted his bike and rode down to the river to eat his lunch. It was cool by the water, and afterwards he dozed a little.

Around mid-afternoon he set off again on a tour of the lanes. He passed the ornate iron gates to Ridgebeck Hall, a tall grey stone house set in rambling grounds.

There were people out walking now, families with small children, all dressed in their Sunday best. He met a pony and trap with some girls aboard, in pretty muslin dresses and bonnets. None had hair the colour of autumn beech leaves and Andy cycled on, disappointed.

Eventually, he went to the farm for his purchases and rode the long miles home. The town was hot and dusty after the fresh green countryside. Andy wondered if he would like to work on a farm like the one he had just visited. It was hard slog, Mam said. But then so was working as a mill hand, and you didn't have the benefits of good clean air and space either.

He felt vaguely depressed, then gave himself a shake. Next Sunday, maybe he'd meet the girl again.

Unhappily for Andy, it didn't happen. Nor the next week. May slipped into June, and every Sunday he made a special effort with his appearance, just in case he met her.

Cottage gardens blazed with colour now, and the fields on the lower slopes of the fells were sweet with new-cut hay. Mrs Whittaker had started putting little treats aside for Mam — a crusty new-baked loaf, a fruit pie, a pot of jam.

"Is she picking up, Andy?" the woman asked kindly, one afternoon towards the end of the month.

"Reckon so." To Andy, Mam had always looked pale and tired, as did most of the other women in the street. A bit of fresh air now and again, and Mam might take on an apple-cheeked look like the woman in front of him.

"Do you like living out here with no other houses around and no neighbours?" he heard himself ask.

She chuckled.

"Bless you, lad, I'm used to it. Though I did enjoy a natter with folks when I had a stall on the market. That all stopped when our Lally married and left home. Lally was the last to go. Bet and Vinnie have been gone ages. No-one at the house to look after things now, see."

Andy had wondered why there was no produce stall on the market. It would have made life much easier for him . . . but then he would not have had the pleasure of his Sunday jaunts.

And he wouldn't have met the girl, a small voice reminded him.

Mrs Whittaker was remarking on the fine weather.

"Just the job for haymaking. I promised Fred a hand getting the bales in. Generally the girls come over and help, but Bet's tied up with the little one now, and the other two couldn't make it this week. Hay has to be got in when it's ready."

"Oh." Next moment, Andy heard himself offering to help.

"I've never worked in the fields before, but I'm strong," he hastened to add.

Andy need not have worried. Mrs Whittaker nodded gratefully, told him to leave his bicycle in the barn and led the way across the yard and over a stile to the fields.

It was back-breaking work, but enjoyable. Andy had never met Farmer Whittaker before. He was a wiry fellow with a droll sense of humour, and loading up the bales on to the wain was done a whole lot faster because he kept them all smiling.

Dusty, hot and sticky, Andy heaved the final bale aboard, flung himself down on top of the sweet-scented hay and watched a sparrowhawk

A FEW Sundays back, just at the beginning of Advent, she noticed a yound husband in church with his two children. As they were strangers in our church, Anne made a point of speaking to them when the service was over.

She congratulated him on the bairns' behaviour. How nice it was to see them at our church — were they on holiday?

She found out they were from Ireland and over to visit friends in the area, just before Christmas. They were charmed when Anne spoke to them.

That Sunday evening, we were in the parlour which Anne had decorated beautifully with lots of holly and ivy and brightly coloured cards from all our friends.

Just before we were about to go to bed, I looked across at Anne in her chair.

"You know," she said, "talking to that Irish family today made me think about Jimmy."

The Farmer And His Wife

weaving lazy circles against the streaky sunset as the horses heaved the cart at a rumbling walk across the shorn fields.

B ACK at the farm, Andy slaked his thirst with home-made ginger beer, and then assisted with the stacking.

"It ain't a job for a novice, this," Farmer Whittaker said. "Hay can go on fire if it's not stacked right. Best you hand me the bales, lad."

Evening was well advanced by the time they had finished. Andy

Should Auld Acquaintance Be Forgot . . .

At New Year, John Taylor takes a moment to remember an old friend.

JIMMY was an Irishman, and when Anne and I were in our teens he was, to our eyes, an old man. I don't suppose he was over sixty.

Jimmy came every year to Anne's farm to help with the hay. He was paid — looking back — in sweeties, but it was his lifeline to take back to Ardban and his dear wife and bairns.

He came across in a cattle boat from Larne to Glasgow. How he got from Glasgow to Fife, Anne can't remember.

After his first meal, he would always ask Anne, "Will you write a letter telling my Marie I'm here?"

Anne added little bits to the letter she thought might interest Jimmy's wife.

Anne had been trying to remember the address he gave her but, as it's more than fifty years past, her memory didn't serve her well.

On the Saturday night, if it was a hay night, he might have driven hay till near midnight, but he was always up at dawn to walk to Mass. Jimmy was a devout Catholic.

He brought his best suit — Anne thinks his only suit — for going to church, and he never had a bite to eat until he got back.

Anne said he was an example to many of us today who, on some Sundays, give church a miss for very flimsy reasons.

Christmas, it seems, is one of the festivals when most of us do make the effort.

Anne said she had no doubt Jimmy would be in Heaven.

He loved his wife and family, he loved his God, and would help any of the farm workers, despite the fact he was dead tired.

Anne went on to say that after she had left home and come to be my wife on the Riggin, Jimmy had worked for her elder brother, Edward, when he had taken over his dad's farm.

Edward had received a note — from one of Jimmy's children — to say he had passed away.

Anne and I had great respect for this Irishman, who had an inner sense of our purpose on earth, which is, Anne says, to serve an apprenticeship for the life to come.

It strikes me that Jimmy would know, too, the true meaning of Christmas.

Thank you, Jimmy, for the memory.

---

retrieved his goods from the dairy where they had been put to keep cool, and went on his way. In his pocket was the money for the milk and eggs, which the couple had returned for a job well done.

"And any time you feel like helping out, lad, you know where to come. Payment in kind of course," was the farmer's parting shot.

Grubby but pleasantly tired, his skin burning from the sun and hay seeds prickling inside his shirt, Andy cycled along. Happen he could manage a few evenings at the farm as well as Sundays, depending on his

The People's Friend Annual

shift at the mill.

Freewheeling down the hill, he started off along the flat and there she was, cycling sedately towards him. Andy wanted the road to swallow him up. After all his effort, here he was looking for all the world like a common farm lad!

She braked, regarding him from under the brim of her straw hat — a boater this time, the purple ribbon around it a perfect match to her ankle-length cycling skirt.

"Good evening," she said. She looked cool and composed and totally beyond his reach.

Andy swallowed hard and mustered a smile.

"Good evening. Grand day it's been. I've been helping get in the hay." Well, he had to make some excuse for his appearance.

She quirked her head impishly.

"That is very clear. I vow half the stack is in your hair!"

Mortified colour stained Andy's cheekbones. He dragged his fingers through his floppy brown thatch.

"They're good sorts at the farm," he burst out defensively. "They've given me extra eggs now for Mam, and there's the chance of work, too."

"Oh? Don't you already have a job?"

"Aye, at Becket's Mill on the road into Burnley. This is extra."

She stared at him.

"You live at Burnley? Dear me, you have come a long way."

"Thirty miles round trip." Andy felt crosser by the minute. "Reckon you're out taking the air again."

"Why, yes. I'm on my way back now." She paused. "Indeed, you do look tired," she said with sympathy.

She smiled, and at once Andy's irritation left him. He mustn't let her vanish again without finding out more about her.

"My name's Edmund Andrew Shannon," he began. It sounded grander than plain Andy, though he had never been called by his full name.

"Pleased to meet you, Edmund Andrew. I'm Evelyn."

"Nice knowing you, Evelyn." He nodded shyly. "Are you heading for Ridgebeck village?"

"Thereabouts. Well, I must be getting along. They'll be watching out for me at the Hall. Goodbye."

SHE pushed off and went sailing effortlessly away up the hill. Andy gazed after her, his heart sinking. So that was it. Daughter of the big house, no less. He might have known.

He set off for home, and somehow the miles seemed twice as long. Reaching the terraced house in the dusty street, he put his bicycle in the shed and took the basket of goods inside.

"You're late!" Daisy said, getting up from the chair by the embers of the fire. "Mam's gone to bed. I said I'd wait up."

Andy looked up sharply.

"Mam's all right?"

"She's fine. This fresh food is doing her good, Andy." Daisy put the metal canister of milk in a pail of cold water to keep cool and took the eggs through to the larder. "Two dozen today!"

"Aye. 'Twas on account of my doing some work for them." Andy's muscles were protesting and his eyelids drooped with sheer fatigue.

"What's wrong, our Andy? Lost a shilling and found sixpence?"

Daisy was next to Andy in age. They had always been very close. He told her about Evelyn.

"Stuck-up thing!" she commented spiritedly when he had finished. "Best forget her. You're worth twenty of her sort!"

"She's real nice. I think she's from the Hall."

"Then she's not for you, Andy."

He shrugged. Daisy might be right, but that did not stop him from dreaming.

THE summer days were long, and since he was on a daytime shift Andy found that if he went straight to the farm after work, he could put in a couple of hours' labour before dusk. He learned how to milk a cow and harness up the horses. He learned how the hay was made, how to tell when the corn was ripe for cutting, and Fred Whittaker promised to teach him to plough. Andy liked the outdoor life.

"We'll make a farmer of you yet," Fred Whittaker joked.

Mrs Whittaker treated Andy to little confidences, like how they'd only had daughters, and Fred would have loved a lad to take over the farm some day. Not that Fred would have a word said against his girls. Loved them to bits, he did. Especially Vinnie, whom he'd spoilt something dreadful! She laughed to take the sting out her words.

She was a friendly, easy-going woman, though Andy was not fooled into thinking she had life easy on the farm. The house was low and sprawling, and keeping it clean was a constant battle.

Andy told the farmer's wife how Daisy was getting married soon and Rose was courting. Daisy's Joe and Rose's William both worked at the mill. Neither of Andy's sisters liked the country, which was just as well since their future seemed destined for the town.

"It can be hard in winter when the snows come down, and we're marooned for weeks. But we cope," the farmer's wife added with a nod.

Andy thought that was what life was all about, coping.

He had seen Evelyn several times on his journeying. Though she always gave him a cheery greeting, never once had she stopped to speak. Probably just as well, Andy supposed, her being gentry.

That afternoon, the weather broke. Thunder crashed overhead and rain hammered on the corrugated iron roof of the shippen as Andy helped Fred Whittaker clean out the byres.

It was still raining when he set off for home. As he neared the flat stretch, he saw a figure trudging through the deluge towards him. It was Evelyn, and she was wheeling her bicycle.

She was soaked, her hat a mess of sodden feathers and silk flowers, her hair darkened with the wet and clinging in rat's tails to her shoulders. For once, they both looked equally dishevelled.

"It's the front wheel," Evelyn said fretfully. "It's jammed. It would happen now in the rain."

"Could be the chain. That's the trouble with these new geared-up chain-drives. Want me to take a look?"

"Oh, please."

With growing respect, she watched as Andy fiddled with the machine and eventually got it working. As he laboured, the rain eased off and the thunder rumbled away.

"Weren't you scared?" Andy asked. "My sisters hate thunderstorms."

"I was more upset over my hat." Evelyn took off the bedraggled article and studied it sadly. "Ruined! Whatever will my mistress say?"

He frowned at her.

"Your mistress?"

"Mmm. I'm maid to Evelyn Myers from the Hall. Miss Evelyn's really kind. She lets me borrow her bicycle and some of her clothes. This is her hat."

"But . . . *you're* Evelyn." The frown deepened.

"Yes, my mistress and I share the same name and the same birthday. And we're both redheads, too! Isn't it fun? 'Course, I'm never called my proper name at home. None of us were. They always got shortened.

"Great pity, since Mother gave us all such beautiful names, too. Loretta got Lally, Elizabetta was Bet, and I was lumbered with Vinnie!" She wrinkled her nose then giggled at Andy's dawning expression.

"Vinnie? You're never Vinnie Whittaker?"

"The very one. And you're Andy."

"Aye, but . . . you knew, and you never said."

"Goodness, I'd have to be very stupid not to have guessed who you were. Mother and Father never stop singing your praises! Andy this, Andy that. I kept hoping you'd turn up at the farm on my day off. I always go home then. I was simply longing to see your face!"

"'Tisn't right, playing tricks on a fellow." He tried to sound cross, but Evelyn — he never would think of her as Vinnie — was looking at him under her long lashes, her mouth curving into a smile and those delicious dimples appearing in her cheeks.

Suddenly, Andy was laughing. And suddenly, the future looked a whole lot more promising all round.

"Here's me thinking you were gentry." He chuckled.

Then he mustered all his courage and asked if she'd go cycling with him next Sunday morning. And to his joy, she accepted with a smile. ❏

I STILL can't believe you're making me do this, Mum." My daughter stood, hands on hips, glaring at me. "It's so uncool to go away with your parents," she went on grumpily. "No-one else does."

For the sake of holiday harmony, I refrained from pointing out that Emma, her best friend, was at this very moment in a plane over the English Channel with her father, and that Lucy was off to Canada next week with her mother and sister.

Rachel sat down on the neat pile of ironed clothes I'd just put on the kitchen chair.

"Of course, it's quite different to go away with one parent, if they're divorced or something. That's cool," she went on.

It was uncanny, the knack she had for knowing how to forestall my arguments even before I'd opened my mouth.

Heading For The Sun

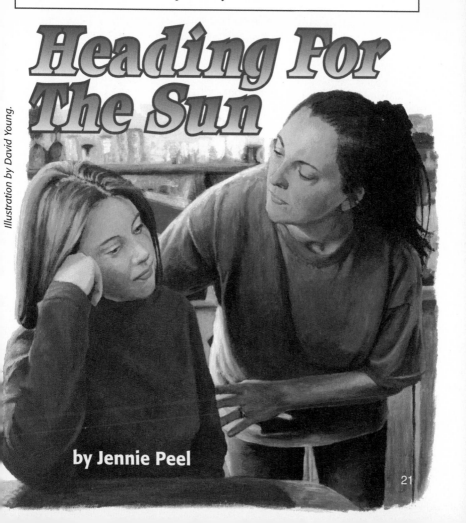

Illustration by David Young.

by Jennie Peel

"Well, I'm sorry that coming from a stable home with two parents who want to take you to Spain is spoiling your street cred," I retorted, feeling my holiday spirit ebbing like the tide.

Rachel rolled her eyes heavenward and got off the chair, knocking the ironing on to the floor as she did so.

"Oh, there's no point in talking to you in this mood. You just don't try to understand." She flounced out of the kitchen, colliding with Robbie as he burst in.

"Out of my way!" she yelled.

"Idiot!" he replied amicably.

"Get a life!" she shrieked, disappearing up the stairs.

"Mum, I can't get these in my case," Robbie said. "Can you put them in yours?"

The bundle of black rubber that he'd been carrying was dumped down on the ill-fated laundry. I picked up something that had once been a flipper. It had a strange grey coating, and part of the webbed foot was torn, making it hang forlornly in my hand.

"Robbie, you really can't take these. They're a health hazard. I thought Dad threw them away ages ago. There's no room in my case, anyway."

"But I'll need them."

"They're too heavy," I told him with a flash of inspiration. "We can only take so much weight on the plane."

"The snorkel's not heavy," he said, picking it up and dangling it under my nose.

I shuddered at the thought of the bacteria-encrusted snorkel being in my case, let alone being used.

"We'll buy you another one when we get there," I promised.

"No, you won't. Dad'll start going on about money growing on trees . . ."

"Well, you're not taking this stuff," I snapped. "It's going in the bin."

"Typical." Robbie groaned. "I don't want to go to Spain anyway. You and Dad will be so embarrassing, drinking too much sangria, dancing about and giggling. It'll be gross."

MY jaw dropped in amazement as he stomped out of the kitchen. It was true Alan and I enjoyed a glass of local wine, and we'd all got a bit hysterical on holiday in Greece when we'd joined in with the traditional folk night.

The sight of my cautious, level-headed husband dancing in a line of men and enthusiastically smashing plates on the floor had been too much for all of us. We'd laughed until our stomachs hurt — Robbie included.

Alan and I had been really looking forward to our family holiday. We realised that, now our children were teenagers, holidays together were soon likely to be a thing of the past.

We'd spent hours poring over brochures, trying to find the ideal package for everyone. Boutiques and night-life for Rachel . . . water ski-ing and other sea sports for Robbie to try.

We'd even hired a car, despite Alan's fears of driving abroad, so we could go out sightseeing if we were unlucky with the weather.

We'd had some wonderful family times in the past although, in the early days, all we could afford was an off-season bargain break. In some ways, those had been the most fun — even when, as so often happened, it was pouring with rain.

We'd explored Cornwall in the rain, thrilled by tales of smugglers and enchanted by the quaint streets and tiny harbours. We'd learned to fish on boat trips in Wales, and spent hours putting coins in amusement arcades on the south coast. We'd all been very proud of the fact that we'd managed to make a small amount of money last so long by choosing our games carefully.

Alan and I looked forward to the day when we could please ourselves and spend hours just sitting by a harbour, or strolling round an ancient ruin, instead of doing everything at our children's hectic pace.

However, we didn't want that time to come just yet and, unlike so many of our friends, we really enjoyed spending some time with our offspring that didn't have to be scheduled into a busy work and home life.

THE sound of Alan's key in the door cut short my reminiscences.

"Are we all packed?" he asked hopefully. As he came into the kitchen he tripped over the pile of rubber and ruined clothes.

"I've had the worst day. First the computer went down, which meant none of the information I'd been working on was available, and then . . ."

"Poor old you," I interrupted, trying to sound sympathetic. "We've nearly finished packing, but I think Robbie would like some help — if you're not too tired."

He looked a little disappointed at the thought of having to get involved and sighed deeply.

"I'll go and see him when I've had a coffee and unwound."

Biting back a comment about how I'd like time to unwind when I got home from work, I just smiled and made the coffee.

My husband laboured under the impression that he was an equal partner in caring for the home and its inhabitants. That was because he put up a shelf about once a year, changed the light bulbs and made sure we had a good supply of toilet paper.

However, after a good deal of sighing and analysing whether a task was really necessary, he would always come to my rescue in a crisis, restoring calm and order to the most troubled waters.

Sure enough, an hour later all the bags were packed — minus the rubber diving gear, which had been safely consigned to the bin. Alan's anxious enquiries regarding an adequate supply of mosquito repellent and suncream had been dealt with.

Whisky Galore!

L ANDING at the cockle beach at Traigh Mhor, it is easy to see why Barra was used as a location for the classic Scottish film "Whisky Galore!". With its gentle rolling hills and spectacular shorelines, the island is enchanting — and most definitely photogenic.

Based on the famous novel by Compton Mackenzie (who also wrote the screenplay, and has a small role in the film as Captain Buncher), "Whisky Galore!" was inspired by a real life incident, which took place in 1941. When the SS *Politician* hit rocks off the coast of Eriskay, the islanders rushed to collect the spilled cargo — thousands of cases of whisky!

It was in 1948 that the film crew and cast — including Gordon Jackson, Jean Cadell and James Robertson Justice — descended on this tiny isle. The islanders soon made them feel welcome — in their own houses, in fact! The actors and production team were put up in the homes of the local people.

Local buildings, such as the schoolhouse, the post office and the bank were used in the filming, and can still be seen today.

Rachel, with the bribe of unlimited shopping in a Spanish market, was resigned to her fate of spending two weeks with the family, and Robbie had overcome his pessimistic view of his father's generosity with the assurance that, once in Spain, he could acquire whatever was needed to become the next Jacques Cousteau.

My feeling of warm admiration for my spouse's diplomatic skills restored my optimism for a happy holiday, and I started feeling quite excited at the thought of clear blue skies and warm sea — not to mention the long, lazy meals that I wouldn't have to cook.

Unfortunately, the feeling vanished when Alan announced that we should go to bed at 8.30 to allow enough time for a good night's sleep.

"Eighty-thirty!" my horrified daughter exclaimed. "I've got loads of emails to send, and my hair to do and . . ."

"I thought you washed your hair yesterday," Alan said, looking puzzled. "It looks very nice."

"Nice!" Rachel shrieked. "Oh, thanks a lot."

"What time are we leaving then, Dad?" Robbie asked suspiciously.

"Four o'clock. So you see, it's important . . ."

Rachel, speechless for once, rolled her eyeballs to show her disgust.

"No way!" Robbie declared. "I bet you've allowed far too much time — as usual."

I hadn't thought it necessary to share our departure time with our children. I'd hoped they wouldn't be with it enough to realise the

On The Silver Screen

Barra's stunning coastline.

pton Mackenzie.

The village hall also served as a temporary studio, when bad weather made filming impossible.

"Whisky Galore!" has remained a timeless classic, loved for its gentle humour, clever story and, of course, its beautiful setting — the real star of the show!

unearthly hour until we were at the airport.

"We don't want to be in a rush, do we? And you don't want to set off tired."

Realising that Alan's voice of reason would probably provoke another mutiny, I smiled at him in what I hoped was an appealing way.

"We'll have plenty of time to catch up on our sleep in the next fortnight, won't we, darling?" I coaxed. "Anyway, I expect they're too excited to sleep."

"All right, I know when I'm beaten," he said, laughing. "But don't let me hear any of you complaining when the alarm goes off."

NEITHER Rachel nor Robbie did complain when the alarm clock went off at three-thirty, because they didn't hear it. However, as Alan, for back-up purposes, had asked for a telephone alarm call, Rachel shot out of bed to answer it after a couple of rings. I never ceased to wonder at the speed of her reaction to the ringing of a phone.

"Some woman asked if I was awake," she told me, sounding annoyed. "I soon put her straight."

Although my sympathies were entirely with the unfortunate operator, I made no comment and bundled my daughter into the bathroom.

Robbie had gone to bed fully clothed and, when pulled out of bed, declared he was ready to go. He then slumped wherever he was put, until he ended up in the car.

The airport was unbelievably busy, and I felt a bit like a sheepdog trying to keep my flock together. I could just imagine Rachel wandering into one of the tempting boutiques and disappearing, or Robbie spotting the internet café, not to mention Alan burying himself in the bookshop.

After standing in the wrong check-in queue for about fifteen minutes, we eventually got to the right place in good time, thereby confirming Alan had been correct to insist that we should leave extra early to allow for just such an eventuality.

Unfortunately, he felt it necessary to point this out and I was desperately trying to think of a way to stop the argument escalating, when I heard a familiar voice behind me.

"I thought it was you!"

Startled, I turned round and was immediately enveloped in a hug by my old friend, Kathy.

Kathy and her family had been our neighbours when our families were little, and we'd been great friends. Sadly, her husband's firm had transferred him to another office and they'd had to move away. We'd kept in touch for a long time and still exchanged Christmas cards and the

Scottish woodland.

occasional telephone call, but we hadn't met for a while.

Our husbands immediately started exchanging anecdotes about the business world.

I turned to Rachel and Robbie.

"You remember Kathy and John, don't you? And their sons, Michael and Ben? You all used to play together."

"Of course," Rachel answered, gazing out from under her eyelashes at Michael and ignoring the others. "How are you?"

Michael, who had been slouching behind his father, hands in pockets, seemed to grow several feet taller.

"OK," he said, running one hand through his spiky dark hair. "It's great to see you again."

Kathy and I started giggling, and I hoped Robbie hadn't noticed this embarrassing parental lapse on my part, but I needn't have worried. He'd found out that Ben still supported the same football team and they were deep in discussion regarding million pound transfer deals and managers that knew nothing!

Bluebell Days

NOW spring, in rainbow robes arrayed,
Paints all the hills with green,
And in the waking woodland glade
Her masterpiece is seen.

Tall saplings rise through pearly mist
Of iridescent blue —
The work of an Impressionist,
Too vibrant to be true!

The artist, from her palette fair,
Has chosen lapis bright,
And ground it to a pigment rare
And blended it with light.

Now, beneath the sunlit trees,
A lake of bluebells gleams;
Its hue as bright as tropic seas
To captivate our dreams!
— *Brenda G. Macrow.*

Sheila D. Taylor.

Kathy and I, both talking at once, soon discovered that not only were we going to the same resort, but the same hotel!

We all had so much to catch up on that, before we knew it, we'd checked in and were waiting in the departure lounge. I looked around at both families. By a wonderful coincidence, this promised to be a great holiday for us all.

I took Alan's hand and squeezed it.

"Just think — a fortnight of sun, sea and sand. Bliss!"

He glanced across at our children, deep in conversation with their new friends, and beamed.

"Happy holiday, darling!" ❑

DID you know that one of your hens is under the strawberry netting?" It was a child's voice, well below my lofty perch on Aunt Em's stepladder in the middle of the forsythia bush. I nearly dropped the secateurs in my hurry to get back to ground level.

"A hen? In the strawberries?"

The child — a little girl of about six or seven, with brown hair neatly tied back and wearing a purple checked dress that had seen better days — beamed up at me.

"It'll be Ermintrude," she said, following me across Aunt Em's garden to the strawberry patch, which had been covered by a green net contraption in an attempt to keep birds out. Sure enough, a small brown hen was pecking around contentedly, her beak a suspicious red colour.

Quickly, I lifted the netting and shooed the hen out into the garden. She gave me an indignant glare and scooted off towards the henhouse.

"She's always doing things like that," the little girl said. "Daddy says she's a positive lia — liability, but I think she's sweet. Who are you?"

Grinning at "Daddy's" description of my aunt's best layer, I secured the strawberry net again.

"I'm Miranda," I told her. "Miss Foster is my Aunt Emily, and I'm looking after her house and garden while she's away. Who are you?"

"I'm Olivia, but Daddy calls me Livvy," my companion said, eyeing the ripe, juicy strawberries with ill-disguised longing on her face. "Are you good at gardens? Miss Foster is. Daddy says she's got green fingers all the way up to her elbows."

That was the problem — I wasn't really a gardening kind of person.

A Family Affair

28

My little balcony at home was covered with shrubs in containers, but that was quite different from Aunt Em's sprawling garden, which at this time of year bore more than a passing resemblance to a flourishing fruit farm.

And I was in sole charge for three months, while lucky Aunt Em was away on the holiday of a lifetime, visiting her sister in Vancouver.

It fitted in well with my own plans. I'd finished one teaching job before the summer holidays, and wasn't due to start the next till October, when I was replacing someone who was having a baby.

So, here I was, gamely trying to keep control of Riverside Cottage and its occupants — Brandy the dog, Timmy and Fudge the cats, and six hens.

"Where do you live?" I asked Olivia, fetching a punnet from the greenhouse and handing it to her. "Would you like to pick some strawberries to take home with you? I'm very grateful you told me about Ermintrude before she ate them all up."

"Oh! Thank you!" Olivia set to work with a will.

"We live down the lane, at number thirty-six," she said over her shoulder. "We haven't been there long. Daddy said we'll have to

by Rosalind Farr

Illustration by Thorsen.

find a nice countryish name for our cottage but we haven't thought of one yet, so it's still just number thirty-six."

"Hm. Difficult," I agreed, hugely entertained. What a lovely little girl she was. Funny and solemn and sweet and helpful — just like I'd want a child of my own to be.

That was why Martin and I had split up. I'd wanted children soon, he'd wanted a career and exotic holidays — and children in about ten years, if at all. Somehow, our two wishes weren't reconcilable. And now that my pride had recovered, I wasn't sorry about splitting up, either.

Olivia stood up, her punnet overflowing and her mouth streaked red.

"I'll take these home now," she said. "We like strawberries. My mummy made strawberry jam once, I think. Are you going to make jam with all of these?"

Aunt Em had left me detailed instructions (she knew me all too well) about both jam-making and fruit-freezing. There were red and blackcurrants, and raspberries, too. And blackberries. Not to mention the plums . . .

I nodded glumly, and watched as Olivia wandered back down the lane, carrying her strawberries carefully. Lucky Mummy and Daddy, I thought, having a daughter like that. Maybe she had brothers and sisters, too.

And here I was, thirty-two next birthday, and still no sign of Mr Right and a proper home and family of my own.

Sighing, I went back to the forsythia.

THAT evening, Brandy and I took our usual before-dinner meander down the lane. I looked at number 36 with interest — this was Olivia's home. It was a five-roomed cottage, like Aunt Em's, but unlike Aunt Em's the front garden consisted of gravel and tubs of various plants. It looked like my kind of garden, though admittedly I couldn't see round the back.

I was still standing there, waiting for Brandy, who had discovered an interesting smell, when Olivia danced out of the front door. A tall, dark man followed her at a more sedate pace.

"Miranda!" she cried, beaming up at me. "We ate *all* the strawberries for lunch.They were lovely. Hello, Brandy!"

She rushed over to the dog. Her father and I watched her, then turned to each other. He had untidy hair and a wonderful lopsided grin, and deep brown eyes that twinkled down at me. Immediately, my heart raced off at top speed.

"Stop it. He's married. You're being juvenile and stupid," a little voice in my head said.

He held out his hand, and I had the presence of mind to shake it.

"You've met Livvy, and I'm Chris," he said. His voice was warm and kind, and little shivers ran up and down my spine. What rotten luck. Here was the man of my dreams, and he was unavailable.

"Olivia was so cute this morning," I told him. "Telling me about Ermintrude, and picking her strawberries. She's lovely."

He was looking at me with a very strange expression on his face.

"Ah, yes, she's a great kid," he said, wiping his forehead with one hand. "Um — would you like to come in for some coffee? Or lemonade? Or — something?"

Startled, I looked at him closely, and noticed that his hands were shaking.

"Oh, I don't want to intrude," I stammered. "Your wife won't want visitors at this time of day. I — "

"I'm not married," he blurted out. "At least, I'm divorced. Livvy's mother moved to America three years ago. Elaine's an actress, quite a good one. Successful. But a country cottage and a family weren't really part of her plans."

A huge wave of happiness swept over me. I smiled at him, suddenly knowing that this was going to be the most special, unforgettable day of my whole life.

"My ex-fiancé went to America last year," I told him. "So I know what it's like."

He nodded, and we both smiled shy, hopeful smiles at each other. Then he led me round the side of the cottage. The back garden was one large patch of grass with an old, gnarled apple tree near the middle. It was definitely my kind of garden.

Chris and I sat down on a little bench by the kitchen window and told each other our life stories while Olivia and Brandy played on the grass. He was a teacher, like me. And we liked similar books and music, though we had different tastes in sport. He was a jogger and I played tennis.

It was weird. I really hadn't believed in love at first sight, but now it was happening to me, and I could see that Chris felt the same way.

"Maybe — I mean — would you come for dinner, some time?" he said hesitantly. "As a 'thank you' for the strawberries? On Friday, maybe?"

I smiled up at him.

"I'd love to," I said happily.

Friday evening saw me ringing Chris's doorbell, feeling quite ridiculously nervous. He opened the door and grinned at me. This was it, I was sure. This was for ever.

The cottage was comfy — soft old armchairs and books all over the place. There was a photo of a younger Olivia with her mother on top of the television, and I looked at it curiously. Elaine was beautiful. But it was me that Chris was looking at with bright, shiny eyes. Me he was chatting away to, obviously enjoying himself. I sighed happily.

And then it all started to go wrong.

I was helping with the salad in the kitchen when Olivia trotted in.

"Oh, good, I like cucumber salad," she remarked, watching as I poured dressing into a bowl.

"My mummy's a great cook," she informed me. "We have lovely meals all together. She can do anything — hamburgers, and pizza. And kebabs."

"Livvy . . ." Chris said, and I could hear helplessness in his voice.

"We have great fun when Mummy comes home," Olivia went on determinedly. "We go to the zoo and for picnics and Mummy makes pizza, and — "

"Livvy, take a bowl of water outside for Brandy," Chris interrupted. "He must be thirsty."

Obediently, Olivia slopped a bowl across the kitchen, and Chris turned to me.

"I'm sorry," he said, his voice trembling. "Livvy can't remember actually living with her mother. She was only three when we split up, and since then they've only been together for a couple of weeks' holiday a year.

"Elaine certainly never produces anything more complicated than a take-away, and she hates zoos and picnics, but — Livvy misses her terribly. She talks about her every day."

He was silent for a moment, then put a hand on my shoulder.

"Livvy has managed to frighten off every woman I've introduced her to, since Elaine left," he said quietly. "Not that there have been dozens, but still. Miranda — "

His eyes were fixed on mine now, and his anguished expression made me want to take him into my arms.

"Miranda, I can feel that this is special. You and me. Please don't let Livvy scare you away, too. She just needs time."

I must admit I was shaken, but I smiled reassuringly and squeezed his hand.

"Don't worry. I'm a teacher, too, remember? It takes more than a six-year-old to frighten me off. Poor little soul, she misses her mother. . ."

Later that evening I walked back along the lane with Brandy, turning at the bend to wave to Chris at the door of number 36. His brief kiss was still warm on my lips, and Livvy's goodnight hug had almost strangled

Crathes Castle, Aberdeenshire

THIS 16th century fairy-tale castle, which took over a century to complete, can be found near the picturesque town of Banchory. Its mediaeval painted ceilings are both colourful and imaginitive, and a delight to visitors.

Equally superb are the castle's fine gardens, constructed by the property's last residents, Sir James and Lady Burnett. Using the tall yew hedges which had been there since the 17th century, they created a series of individual plots, each with its own theme.

With so many fine features, it's no wonder that this spectacular castle is one of the National Trust for Scotland's busiest attractions.

CRATHES CASTLE, ABERDEENSHIRE: J. CAMPBELL KERR

me. Maybe everything would be all right . . .

And in one sense, everything was more than just all right. The long summer days passed in a mixture of working in the garden, exploring the countryside and falling completely and crazily in love. I was happier than I'd ever been before, and I could tell that Chris was happy, too. It was a wonderful, never-ending summer.

But Livvy — it was strange. She was obviously very fond of me, rushing up for a kiss whenever I arrived, and hugging me tightly when I left, but — she just wouldn't stop talking about her mother.

Every time I visited their cottage — which was nearly every day, after the first few weeks — she produced another story of family life with Mummy and Daddy.

I found it really quite difficult. It was hurtful to hear about the man that I loved gallantly holding an umbrella over Mummy at the zoo, or being beaten at family hide and seek, thanks to Mummy cleverly finding him in the kitchen cupboard.

Chris and I were very careful to include Livvy in all our outings. I didn't want her to feel that she was being pushed aside in any way. But even when she was obviously thoroughly enjoying herself, it was never long before she started off on another "Mummy" story.

At the Dinosaur Theme Park — Livvy's "end of the summer hols" treat — I really thought we'd cracked it. Livvy was so happy, laughing with us both, all hugs and kisses — and I got more of these than Chris. But then, on the way home, she started.

"It's fun like that all the time with Mummy here," she told me sleepily. "Families are the best thing of all, don't you think?"

Her eyes closed then, and Chris and I looked at each other. What on earth were we going to do?

As it happened, the decision was taken out of our hands. The next day I was going to town to help a friend celebrate her thirtieth birthday. It was late before I let myself into Aunt Em's cottage, where Timmy and Fudge greeted me rapturously. Brandy was boarded out with Chris and Livvy.

Exhausted, I fell asleep as soon as my head touched the pillow.

A distant banging sound woke me, and slowly I realised it was someone knocking on the door. I looked at the clock. Half past four. What on earth . . ?

IT was Livvy, still in pink pyjamas and Barbie slippers. "Daddy's got a sore tummy and I can't find the medicine!" she wailed. "And he can't get up. Oh, please help!"

"I'll be there in two minutes," I said, grabbing my jeans.

One look at Chris's grey, crumpled face and I dialled 999.

"It started yesterday morning," he told me, his voice hoarse. "Just the odd twinge. Then suddenly it got worse. Probably appendicitis."

The paramedics agreed with this diagnosis, and bundled Chris

34

efficiently into the ambulance.

"Stay here with Livvy," he groaned, and I nodded, though I wanted more than anything to go with him and stay as close by him as they'd let me.

But Livvy needed me. She was shaking all over, and her eyes were huge. I made hot chocolate and sat cuddling her in the living-room.

"Is my daddy going to die?" she whispered as I rocked her.

"Oh, darling, people don't die of appendicitis," I said heartily, trying to convince myself, too. "Daddy'll be fine. And — and you have Mummy, too, don't you?"

Elaine's photo smiled down on us from the television. Livvy was silent, and then she looked up at me.

"Mummy's not here," she said flatly. "She's not like a proper mummy, she only comes sometimes on holiday. I wish you were my mummy, Miranda. You and me and Daddy have such good times, don't we?"

Two tears trickled down her face, and I hugged her tightly, pondering. Had Chris and I got hold of completely the wrong end of the stick?

"Livvy," I said at last. "Tell me, why did you always talk about the good times you had with your mummy?"

"I wanted you to stay," she said. "I thought if you knew how much fun it was with a mummy and a daddy and me, then you'd stay and be my mummy. You're so nice and I do want a real mummy."

"Oh, sweetheart!" There was nothing I could do except cuddle her, and presently she fell asleep. I put her back to bed and made coffee.

At eight o'clock the phone rang, and I felt justified in waking Livvy to tell her the good news.

"Daddy's had his operation — it *was* appendicitis," I said. "And everything's fine. He's sleeping now but we'll go and visit him after lunch. OK?"

We took flowers and grapes to the hospital, and I managed to tell Chris about Livvy's confession while she was arranging the flowers at the table.

He grinned.

"I must be very stupid," he said, taking my hand in both his own. "But you'll marry me anyway, won't you?"

"You bet," I said, accepting what had to be the most unromantic proposal of all time. "Livvy, how would you like to be a bridesmaid?"

It was the most wonderful wedding I could ever have imagined. Sunshine, flowers, church bells — nothing could have been more perfect. Livvy stayed with Aunt Em while we went on our honeymoon, and when we arrived back home we discovered that our family had grown.

"Aunt Em's given me Ermintrude," Livvy informed us happily. "After all, it was Ermintrude who started everything off, wasn't it? And can we buy some friends for her — oh, and some strawberry plants, too? And rasps?"

Chris and I looked at each other over her head.

"Anything you like, darling," I said. "We'll all muck in and help. After all, we're a family now, aren't we?" ❑

A Word Of Advice

THOSE roast potatoes were lovely, Susan." My mother-in-law, Daisy, smiled warmly at me as she helped to clear the dishes from the table. I tensed.

"But I was just wondering," Daisy continued, as I had known she would, "have you ever tried shaking the pan before you put them in the oven? It makes the world of difference."

"I'm sure it does, Daisy," I replied, trying to sound cheerful. "I'll remember to try it next time."

Daisy beamed, making me feel even more wretched. On the surface, of course, Daisy and I seemed to get along wonderfully. But the deeper, more intimate relationship, the kind of mother-daughter relationship I had always hoped to have with her, had never developed.

With more effusive compliments on the Sunday dinner I'd prepared, Daisy kissed both Mike and me goodbye. Then she revved her Mini and hurtled down the lane at breakneck speed.

"I wish she'd drive a little slower," Mike said, as he stood in the doorway, watching his mother's car disappear around the bend. It was what he said every Sunday when she came to dinner.

He turned back to help me with the washing-up.

"Well? What was it this time?"

"The potatoes." I sighed and handed him a plate.

It was always something, you see. Ever since Daisy and I first met, she had offered me advice. Friendly, cheerful advice, usuall accompanied by a long, prattlin tale of her own experience.

At first, I was grateful for it. hoped it was the beginning of wonderful relationship. But after while . . . well, I began to wonde Was I doing everything wrong Pretty soon, I began to take wha was no doubt kindly advice a constant criticism.

My own mother had died when was a baby, and my father and I ha never been particularly close. So I' been terribly excited when Mik and I had got engaged, thinking tha at last I might have the kind c

by **Katharine Swartz**

nother-daughter relationship I had always longed for . . . lots of heart-o-heart talks and laughter, the kind of warmth and closeness I had never been able to have with my own mother.

At first, it seemed like it might happen. Daisy was bright, funny, cheerful — and full of advice! I

began to realise that, kind and well-meaning as she might be, we just didn't click. I started to resent her advice, and dread her visits.

There was the time we were redecorating our house. First, Daisy offered to paint our sitting-room for us, since she had so much experience. A very kind offer, I

37

know, but as a young wife and first-time home owner, I wanted to paint the room myself.

To compromise, I asked Daisy if she would help me paint it. What a mistake! I spent a miserable two days listening to her advice on everything from how to open the paint cans to what the best brush strokes were and how to clean the brushes.

By the end, the sitting-room walls were a beautiful pale blue, but I was a nervous wreck.

And everything was like that. A visit didn't go by without Daisy offering me her kindly advice on some topic.

And now that I was expecting our first baby, I knew Daisy, mother of four, would have advice aplenty!

As if reading my thoughts, Mike put his arms around me.

"It's not your fault the two of you don't click," he said. "That's just the way it is, sometimes."

"I know." I sighed. But it was still a disappointment.

Mike rested his hands on top of my swelling bump.

"Are you sure you're going to be all right with me going away next week?" he asked anxiously. He'd been asking me this same question for days, ever since he found out he had an urgent business trip to Belgium.

"I'll be fine," I reassured him once again. "I'm only thirty-six weeks along. There's no need to worry."

"That's how you've always been, Sue. Do everything yourself, your own way. It's why you and Mum don't get along. But I still worry."

Mike was right, I thought later, as I soaked in the tub. I did like to do things my way, even if it meant making mistakes.

So why didn't I tell her? I had often thought about doing that, but I knew Daisy meant well, and I didn't want to hurt her feelings.

No doubt Daisy had some gripes about me, too. She might well wish I didn't insist on doing things my own way so much.

I sighed and stepped out of the tub. No, unfortunate as it was, Daisy and I were just too different. We were destined to stay as we were — polite and kind to one another, no more.

THE next week, while Mike was away, I busied myself with all the chores I hadn't managed to do in ages. I had left work several weeks earlier, but still hadn't managed to get the baby's room in order. I was deep into dusting when I felt the first twinge. No, I thought, it couldn't be.

I continued dusting, and the twinges continued twingeing.

After an hour or so, I started timing them. Ten minutes apart. It had to be false labour, I thought. I was still weeks away from my due date!

By this time, the twinges were becoming decidedly uncomfortable, and I knew I needed to do something. If only Mike were here!

I groaned inwardly. The only thing to do was telephone Daisy. I could have rung one of my friends, but most of them were at work. And I knew in my heart it was unfair to exclude Daisy from the possible birth of her grandchild.

But this was one time, I thought, when I really, really did not want her advice! If Daisy advised me on how to roast potatoes, I could just imagine how much she'd have to say about giving birth!

* * * *

I hung up the phone with a long sigh. Daisy had promised to come straight over. Part of me was relieved, but another part dreaded her arrival. That was unfair, I knew, because Daisy had never been anything but helpful — in her own way.

By the time she did arrive, I was surprisingly grateful to see her. I was feeling quite uncomfortable by then, and the sight of Daisy's familiar Mini hurtling up our lane almost reduced me to tears. I think I wouldn't have minded some of her advice then, but for once, amazingly, she didn't give any.

"I'll make you a nice cup of tea and we'll ring the hospital," she said with brisk efficiency as she bustled into the kitchen. "Have you packed a bag?"

I nodded, sinking into a chair.

"Don't you worry. You're doing wonderfully."

Daisy rang the hospital and explained my condition while I sipped gratefully at a cup of hot tea.

"Right," she said as she hung up the phone. "The midwife thinks you should go straight in."

"Already?" My nerves were getting the better of me. "I thought your first child was supposed to take ages!"

"Perhaps you're lucky," Daisy replied with a smile. "Shall we go in my car?"

I could imagine Mike's dismay at hearing that Daisy was to drive me at her usual breakneck speed, but at this point I was just glad to be going to the hospital as quickly as possible.

The next few hours passed in a blur, but I did remember Daisy sitting next to me, holding my hand and whispering encouraging words.

When I felt like I couldn't go on any longer, Daisy told me she knew I could. And not one word of advice passed her lips!

Afterwards, as I held my daughter in my arms, I smiled my gratitude.

"Daisy, I don't know what I would have done without you," I said. "Really."

Daisy smiled wryly, brushing one fingertip against the baby's soft cheek.

"It's probably the first time that's happened."

"What do you mean?"

"Oh, I know it hasn't been easy between us," Daisy explained, her voice tinged with wistful sadness.

"I realised soon after you married Mike that you probably didn't appreciate all my prattling advice. And I must say, I don't blame you. I've always wanted to do things my own way, too . . . whether it was decorating the house, cooking my own meals or finding my own job!"

I could hardly believe what Daisy was saying.

"The truth is, we should have had this conversation ages ago, but I was always afraid to bring it up," she continued.

"Me, too," I admitted.

"It wasn't until now, seeing you with your daughter, that I knew I had to say something. I want us to have a new beginning, for all of our sakes." She nodded towards my daughter, and I felt a huge lump in my throat.

"I didn't realise you knew how I felt," I said quietly. It was a wonderful relief finally to admit my true feelings to Daisy. "I always meant to take your advice . . ."

"Oh, Susan." Daisy shook her head. "When I was young, I didn't want some old biddy telling me what to do. I wanted to find out for myself."

"You're hardly some old biddy!" I protested, laughing. "Especially when you roar around in your Mini!"

Daisy laughed, too.

"The trouble is, we're just too alike. I was just like you when I was younger, and I've learned from the mistakes I made. I just want to share that with you — but I suppose we all have to make our own mistakes."

Tears stung my eyes. I had never seen it that way. Rather than being too different, we were too similar! Like a real mother and daughter . . .

All of a sudden, Daisy's advice didn't seem so frustrating. In fact, I thought I might begin to appreciate some help from a woman who was obviously so wise.

"I'm going to need some advice when it comes to this little one," I said, nestling my daughter close. "I'm an absolute beginner where motherhood is concerned!"

"You'll do fine," Daisy assured me. "But I'm sure I won't be able to resist adding my bit now and again, if you don't mind."

"I don't," I said. "Not any more."

Now that there was this new honesty between us, I knew I could listen to Daisy's advice with gladness, and sometimes even follow it!

Just then, Mike rushed in, a shadow of stubble on his face, his eyes anxious.

"I got here as soon as I could!" He stopped in his tracks at the sight of me, with the baby in my arms.

"Meet your daughter," I said with a smile.

Mike took the baby in his arms and gazed at her in wonder.

"She's a miracle," he whispered.

I smiled at Daisy.

Two miracles had happened here today. I had gained a mother as well as a daughter.

Gazing at Mike, the baby and Daisy, I knew I had all I could ever want. ❑

On The Beach

A COLD, wet nose snuffling in her ear wasn't the way Miranda generally chose to greet the new day. In fact, if the truth were told, she tried *not* to greet it. Even on workdays, she'd wait until the last possible minute before stumbling out of bed.

She only surfaced when the important matter of what to wear needed her attention. Then she had breakfast on the run. And, of

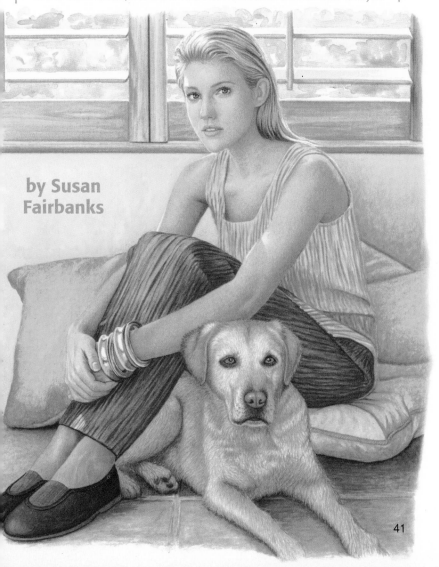

by Susan
Fairbanks

41

course, she always left it too late to catch the bus to the city. Which meant driving her car into Adelaide and paying for all-day parking.

One day . . . one day she would rise far enough in the company to stroll in at ten and have her own parking space, but until then . . .

"Go away," she muttered when the snuffling became impossible to ignore. She pulled the pillow over her head in an attempt to deflect the wet nose, and to hide from the early morning light.

She'd come home late last night and crawled into bed without switching on the light, leaving the curtains open. Her clothes were where she had abandoned them, strewn across the floor. What a slob she was!

Archie, she remembered, had been sulking in his basket in the laundry and hadn't bothered to greet her. He was still cross that his owner had apparently abandoned him yesterday to a very indifferent dogsitter.

Archie seemed to have shrugged off his grouchiness this morning. Once he had established Miranda was awake, he jumped up on her bed, his golden body wriggling with delight at this new game of hide-and-seek, his tail waving enthusiastically.

Defeated, Miranda rolled on to her back and groped for her alarm clock. Six o'clock! She groaned and tried to pull the sheet up over her face, but Archie pounced, plonking himself firmly across her.

Although he was only a medium-sized dog, he was too heavy to ignore. He tried to lick her chin.

"Get down, you wretched dog!" She struggled upright, pushing him away. He sat on the end of the bed, poised for the next move, head cocked to one side and tail thumping loudly against the bedstead.

It was all too much, too early. Miranda looked at him resentfully as she swung her legs over the edge of the bed.

Her brother had promised that looking after Archie for a few days would be no trouble.

"Just feed him and take him for W-A-L-K-S — don't say the word out loud, he barks if he hears it," Paul had said.

He hadn't mentioned anything about early mornings, with the expectation of a W-A-L-K. This did not augur well for the rest of the week.

Miranda had expected the Esplanade to be deserted at six-thirty on a weekday morning, but the beachfront, when she arrived, was alive with people. Power walkers came striding past looking serious. Joggers gave her a brief smile as they sweated on their way, knowing she wasn't one of them.

Miranda looked away guiltily as Archie tugged her along on his lead. She'd been meaning to do something more ambitious than her weekly half-hearted effort in the gym, but then . . .

And there were people actually swimming! It was still only spring, and the South Australian waters hadn't had the benefit of any really hot weather to take the edge off the chill. But there they were, floating happily on the waves.

"Fancy joining us?" An elderly man came up to her as she stood on the

Esplanade, watching the swimmers. "We swim here every day."

Miranda gave an involuntary shiver.

"Maybe when it's a bit warmer," she said, trying not to sound too faint-hearted.

"We swim all year, you know." The man bent to unchain his bicycle from a railing. "We call ourselves the Somerton Icebergers. We've been going for over twenty years." He adjusted his helmet.

"You'd be very welcome — no joining fee!"

"Thank you." Miranda smiled weakly as she watched him cycle away.

An impatient tug reminded her of why she was there. Archie was pulling her towards the beach, where six or seven dogs of different shapes and sizes were running on the sand.

One man had been throwing a ball for his cattle dog, but it was clear who had grown tired of the activity first. The ball now lay on the ground while the dog crouched expectantly at his owner's feet.

Archie looked longingly in their direction, but Miranda didn't dare let him off the lead. She was also regretting she hadn't taken more care with her appearance before they set out.

The man with the cattle dog looked rather nice — about her age, early thirties, perhaps, with a pleasant face, fit and tanned.

Just her luck to spot an interesting-looking man when she was wearing a tracksuit with baggy knees and elbows and last night's mascara.

THE tide was halfway out, leaving a wide stretch of firm, damp sand over which seagulls were wandering in search of food. Archie decided the gulls needed rounding up, so he and Miranda set off in hot pursuit, with no hope of ever achieving anything other than wet, sandy feet. And a stitch in Miranda's side.

"Enough!" she cried breathlessly, when it seemed as though Archie wanted to run all the way to Glenelg Jetty. The gulls had long since flown away. "It's all very well for you, Archie. I've got to go to work, while you have the rest of the day to lie around and recover."

She glanced at her watch. Nearly an hour before she would normally have got out of bed! If they jogged back along the beach, she would even have time to have a proper breakfast, which her mother was always nagging her about, and catch the bus.

Thursday morning wasn't so . . . interesting. Archie proved to be an unreliable timekeeper. Miranda wasted even more time deciding what to wear, and trying to find a matching band for her hair, so it was a quarter past seven by the time they arrived on the Esplanade.

The Icebergers had already emerged from the sea and were standing around chatting, but the man with the cattle dog was nowhere to be seen. Maybe he and his dog had already been and gone.

The elderly man from yesterday gave her a friendly wave. Miranda waved back but kept on walking, dragging along a reluctant Archie, who wanted to go the other way.

He had spotted a small black dog nearby, carrying a stick in its mouth and refusing to give it up to its owner — obviously an Archie sort of game. She would have to bring something to throw.

Setting the alarm for six o'clock on Friday would have seemed unthinkable a week ago. So, too, would going to bed early.

She had even turned down an invitation for drinks after work. One of her female colleagues belonged to a singles club and they were meeting in a city cocktail bar this week. Miranda had been to several of their events before, but had never met anyone who'd attracted her enough to meet again for a date.

"You're too fussy!" her friend had said. "You always want an expert in art, current affairs, literature and music, all rolled into one. It scares them off."

Miranda grimaced.

"You're probably right," she agreed ruefully. "I'll come with you next week. It's a French film, isn't it? I'm babysitting my brother's dog this week, and I'm scared Archie will eat the rugs or dig up the pot plants if I leave him too long."

FRIDAY morning was full of promise. It was a glorious, sunny start to the day, the air still fresh from the night, but with a hint of warmth to come.

Miranda felt confident enough by now to let Archie off his lead once they were on the beach. As soon as he was free he charged off after the seagulls, splashing through the shallows, never quite close enough to catch any of the birds, but seeming to enjoy himself anyway. He rushed back to Miranda, tongue lolling out the side of his mouth in a canine grin.

The elderly man had just arrived for his swim and came across to where Miranda was paddling.

"You're early this morning," he said, smiling. "Your dog seems to be enjoying himself."

Miranda had made an interesting discovery. In the three days she had been walking Archie, people who would have otherwise kept their heads down

Gordon Lyon.

44

and hurried on took the time to stop and say hello, and pat her dog.

"This is Archie's first holiday at the beach," she explained. "He obviously doesn't know much about birds, but he's getting plenty of exercise."

"Oh! Betty thought you were a local girl — she's one of our group, the lady in the blue costume. I'm Tom, by the way." He held out his hand.

"Miranda." She shook his hand. "Yes, I am. Local, I mean, if you count three years as local. I live a couple of blocks back from the beach. Archie's on loan from my brother, who's away at the moment."

"Betty thought she'd seen you before — pruning roses."

"Oh. Was she the kind lady who came to my rescue? I didn't know how much to cut off. I'm not very good at gardening!"

"Come and be properly introduced to her. She's here with her husband and one of her neighbours who swims with us. They haven't got into the water yet." Tom seemed keen for her to meet everyone and Miranda smiled.

"As long as it's obligation free!" she said. "I'm a chicken when it comes to swimming any time before summer."

She followed her new friend over to the group who were placing their belongings on the rocks, out of reach of the tide.

"What a nice dog you have!" Betty said. Archie had come bounding over and was lapping up the attention as people patted him. "What breed is he?"

Season Of Light

IN nets of golden foliage bright
The trees have trapped the dancing light.
And leafy shadows all around
Cast dapples on the mossy ground.
Such beauty makes the spirit whole,
Brings comfort to the troubled soul,
And tells us, when the days are grey,
That spring is never far away.
And we, in thought, can yet return
To scenes for which our hearts still yearn,
And see the beeches, lately bare,
Flutter their leaves in sunlit air,
While scented breezes softly sing
Their love songs to returning spring!
— *Brenda G. Macrow.*

Loch Oich, Invergarry.

"My brother likes to claim he's an Old Australian Sheepdog when anyone asks," Miranda said. "He's a sort of Labrador cross — Paul got him from the Lonsdale Animal Shelter about a year ago."

There was a general chat about the heartlessness of people who abandon their pets, when Miranda suddenly caught sight of a cattle dog running into the surf after a ball.

She excused herself from the friendly group, recklessly promising to swim with them in December (it would be summer then, after all!), before trying to convince Archie he should start chasing things into the sea. She just needed the chance to, oh, so casually, return any stray balls that Archie happened to find. To the thrower. Suitably apologetic, of course . . .

Unfortunately for Miranda's fantasy, Archie had spotted four or five gulls in the opposite direction, and took off after them. She was forced to follow, with a wistful glance over her shoulder as the man and his dog receded into the distance.

Paul rang from Jakarta that evening. In fact he woke her up, and she grumbled at the late call.

"Have I got the time wrong? I deliberately tried not to ring in the middle of your favourite television programme!"

Miranda looked at the clock. It was true. In the Good Old Days (last week) she would probably have been sprawled out on the sofa at this time, with a drink in one hand and the remote in the other, trying to decide whether to watch the late-night movie.

"Sorry," she mumbled, shifting the handset to the other ear. "I went to bed early. How are things going?"

"Very well." Paul sounded happy. "I should be home on time, so I'm checking if it's still OK for you to meet me at the airport on Sunday evening?

"Great. The other reason I phoned — I was wondering how you're getting on with Archie. I felt a bit guilty afterwards, leaving him with you, when I knew you didn't really want him. But he was so miserable when I left him in the kennels last time."

"I know, and we're getting on fine. In fact —" Miranda hesitated. "In fact, I was wondering if I could keep him a bit longer?"

There was silence at the other end.

"How long is a bit longer?" Paul's voice sounded odd.

"I don't know. A couple of days, perhaps. It depends."

"You'd better tell me what's going on. I'm not sure I want my dog being involved in something shady."

He was definitely laughing now, and Miranda wasn't sure how she could explain.

"Well, there's this . . . No." She paused, then tried again. "You know how everyone stops to talk to you when you're walking a dog?"

"Not if it's a Rottweiler baring its teeth!" her brother retorted.

"You know what I mean," Miranda said impatiently. "Anyway. There's this — interesting-looking man who walks his dog on the beach at about six-thirty in the morning."

"In the *morning*?" Paul said incredulously. "You've been up walking Archie at six-thirty?"

Miranda ignored him.

"I'd rather like to meet him, and Archie seems the best way to engineer it. Though he's let me down so far," she added wryly.

"This all sounds a bit hare-brained to me. Typical Miranda, I might add. How do you know this bloke's not already spoken for? Archie could be barking up the wrong gum tree!"

She had to wait until Paul stopped laughing at his own joke before she could reply.

"I'm only suggesting talking to him, for heaven's sake, not eloping. How else do you get to find out anything about anyone?"

"You're looking for a dream man who doesn't exist, and at your age, Miranda, you can't be too choosy," her unsympathetic brother said. "You're too fussy."

"Not you, too." Miranda sighed. "I'm not looking for perfection. I'd just like to find a man with similar interests and values, who laughs at the same things I do. Someone I can share my life with. You, of all people, should appreciate that!"

Was that below the belt? Paul was still sensitive about his break-up last year . . .

They agreed to discuss the Archie question again on Sunday when Miranda collected Paul from the airport. Who knew, Paul suggested, signing off — if her tactics were successful, Archie might have a whole new future. They could be on to a perfect money spinner — Archie the Matchmaker!

THE problem about Saturday was: would people who took their dogs for walks before work during the week continue with the same timetable at the weekend? Or would people take advantage of a lie in?

In the end, Archie elected for the early start, and Miranda rolled out of bed as though she had been doing it for years.

A quick splash of water on her face — no trace of yesterday's make-up these days — a touch of lip gloss and a glance in the mirror at today's outfit and they were on their way.

"Now, Archie, this may take a while. It's time you did some serious training." Miranda had remembered to bring a tennis ball this time.

It was another beautiful day, the cool morning air inviting early risers to step out briskly. Even the Icebergers' ranks had swelled.

Miranda had stopped to talk to Tom and the others, who invited her to a pre-Christmas breakfast on the foreshore.

"A chance for everyone to get to know one another." Betty smiled. "We ask all the beachgoers around here."

Highlander

Eilean Donan.

On The Silver Screen

Dennis Hardley.

Could she drop a hint about a particular man and his dog? But Miranda resisted the temptation. It would be too embarrassing if he turned up with his wife and five children in tow.

Archie took to his training like a natural, chasing and returning the ball with great enthusiasm.

True, there was the unfortunate incident in the shape of a Chihuahua, where Archie's innocent greeting was misconstrued. Archie retreated with a sharp yelp, but no lasting harm was done.

The Chihuahua's owner apologised to Miranda for her pet's hostile reception.

"I'm afraid she sees any dog larger than a thimble as a threat," the woman explained, tucking her dog under her arm.

"When you're that small, it's understandable." Miranda gave Archie a consoling pat. "Archie's not streetwise yet. He loves everybody."

Apart from that, training continued without interruption. Archie retrieved and dropped the ball at Miranda's feet with mind-numbing regularity. She could see why the human half of this game always wanted

AS one of the most photographed castles in Scotland, it is hardly surprising that Eilean Donan should become the star of a Hollywood movie. Indeed, it has much in common with the film in which it appears. Like the film, "Highlander", Eilean Donan represents a romanticised idea of the Highlands, with its clansmen, myths and superstitions.

In fact, the castle was completely rebuilt during its restoration — which began in 1912 and finished some twenty years later — from a pile of rubble, with little idea of what the original fortress looked like.

In the movie, which was made in 1986, the castle is referred to as Glamis Castle, which is actually just outside Dundee — some miles away from Loch Duich.

Under a stormy sky, the warrior Highlanders of the film — including the actor Christopher Lambert — set out for battle from the castle, just as the movie's producers imagined the real mediaeval highlanders had once done.

Sean Connery and Christopher Lambert.

Appropriately, Scotland's famous son, Sean Connery, appears in the film — though he plays a Spaniard! — and the far-fetched tale of immortality, magical sword fights and ancient destinies unfolds in spectacular fashion.

to stop first.

So far they had only practised on the flat, sandy beach. Miranda needed to make sure Archie knew what was what before advancing to the wet stage.

"Here goes, Archie!" She held the ball up so he could see it, and then hurled it into the sea as far as she could.

Archie just stood and looked.

"Go and get it, then," she said encouragingly. The ball was bobbing up and down on the waves, clearly visible from the shore.

Archie just stood and barked.

The ball bobbed and started to drift with the outgoing tide.

"Come on, Archie. Fetch it!" Miranda pulled off her trainers and waded into the water.

Archie watched her, and barked.

Miranda waded a little deeper, hoping her expensive new shorts wouldn't get too splashed with the salt water.

Archie ran up and down at the edge of the water, looking at her

49

anxiously, and continuing to bark.

Could it be that Archie couldn't swim? Miranda had just assumed all dogs could swim. Doggy-paddle, and all that. Perhaps if she grabbed him and carried him out of his depth, he would just take to it . . . like a duck to water . . .

Something in her manner must have alerted Archie. As soon as she approached, he scampered off, just out of reach. This was a new game, splashing in and out of the shallows, ducking and weaving, kicking up sand and sea-water.

Miranda made a feint to the right, and managed to catch Archie as he brushed past her legs on the left.

"Got you!" she cried triumphantly, grabbing hold of him while he kicked and wriggled, managing to lick her face at the same time.

"Is this what you were after? I saw you trying to get your dog to retrieve it."

The man with the cattle dog stood in front of her, holding a wet tennis ball. He looked even nicer in close-up mode.

"I'm afraid Barney can't resist chasing balls, so he went after it."

"Barney?" she said stupidly, still hanging on to Archie, who was now madly wagging his tail.

It wasn't supposed to happen like this, with sand all over her and her shorts flapping wetly around her legs, she thought numbly.

"My dog. To have a barney: have a blue — Aussie slang for argument? He's a Blue Heeler, you see." The cattle dog's owner looked slightly embarrassed at the explanation. "He'll chase balls all day, even ones that don't belong to him."

"That's really clever — Barney for blue, I mean. It took us ages to think of a name for Archie." Was she gabbling? She took a deep breath.

"Thank you for bringing the ball back. I didn't realise Archie couldn't swim."

"He probably can, but perhaps he's not used to the sea." The man smiled at her. "I don't think I've seen you here before this week, have I? Walking your dog?"

So he'd noticed, had he? You never would have guessed.

"No. This is the first week I've had Archie. I'm looking after him for my brother."

His smile broadened.

"Why don't you let Archie go?" he suggested. "He can play with Barney for a while. And since they're getting acquainted, I should introduce myself. I'm Simon Bennett."

His handshake was firm, but not so as to break any fingers. Miranda wondered how soon it would be before it would be polite to ask about a wife and five children. After all, some things have to be clarified before a relationship can advance.

But somehow, she had a feeling Archie had done his job . . . ❏

In The Same Boat

P ARIS," Simon said as he reached into the depths of the boat for the bailer, "got lucky. He might have fought a ten-year war, but at least he got the Helen who launched a thousand ships."

"While you got the Helen who sank them!" Helen wasn't exactly happy about being stuck in the middle of a boating lake with wet feet, but she could still just about see the funny side.

"Anyway, you were the one who chose the boat," she pointed out.

"I liked the name!" Simon said defensively, and she gave up and smiled.

As romantic dates went, it got "A" for effort, and "E" for

by Tia Brown

achievement. And that, she realised, leaning back and enjoying the sunshine, had summed up their relationship right from the start.

Murphy's law could have been written just for Simon Murphy . . .

They'd met at the garage; two tormented souls whose cars had just failed their MOTs so drastically that they'd need second mortgages to repair them. Their eyes had met over the report forms as they'd sunk into the chairs the garage had thoughtfully provided for its stunned victims.

"Bet mine's longer than yours," he'd said, but she'd been in no mood for funnies. She'd been too busy debating the rival merits of sucking up to bank managers with the temperament of hungry wolves, not eating for a month, or learning to love walking everywhere.

"I don't even know what a steering rack is," he'd gone on, as if he hadn't noticed that she wasn't listening.

"Expensive."

She knew that all too well, because hers had gone, too.

"But not as expensive as a clutch," Simon had continued gloomily.

"But dearer than new windscreen wipers."

Helen could have kicked herself for not checking those, but it wouldn't have made much difference to the outcome. Her car was about as failed as it was possible to be. Then she glanced at his list, and felt a little better; it was at least six lines longer.

"I'm going to need time to think about this," she told the mechanic.

"Me, too. It might be cheaper to throw the car away and start again," his voice had chimed in, and they'd walked together to pick their cars up.

"The stupid thing is," he'd said as they walked, "it was running fine. Better than it ever had."

"As far as you could tell," Helen had corrected him. "But think of the accident you could have had. Middle of a motorway at rush hour, go to pull into the fast lane, the steering goes, and there you are on the nine o'clock news as the cause of a fifteen car pile-up."

"Are you always this optimistic?" he'd asked, and she'd noticed that he had a really great grin.

"No, sometimes I'm a real pessimist."

She'd looked at her car, and had known that now was one of those times. It still looked much the same, but she had to face facts. It was unsafe.

IT'LL be all right," he'd said, much to Helen's surprise.

"How can you tell?"

"Things usually are. Darkest hour just before dawn; when God closes a door, He opens a window and all that . . . And no, I'm not a human fortune cookie." He produced that grin again, but it faded as he looked at his own car.

"Goodness knows where I'm going to get the cash for this," he muttered, and things had gone on nicely from there.

They'd stood, leaning against their cars in the August sunshine, discussing the unfairness of life in general and ungrateful cars in particular, and when she saw him at the garage the following day, she greeted him as if he was an old friend.

"Well? Will it live?" he'd asked.

"I went to see the bank." She sighed.

"Mortgaged your soul to the evil empire?" he asked with a grin, and she struggled not to laugh.

"What have you got against banks?" she asked.

"I work for one." The one he worked for turned out to be hers, and he'd looked at her lending application, which meant he knew far too much about her, which wasn't fair.

On the other hand, he did have his name badge on so she knew he was Simon Murphy, and he, too, had decided to take the gamble and have the work done.

"Fingers firmly crossed that nothing else falls off. Mind you, I'm not sure there is anything that's not on the list."

"There is, believe me," she said fervently, because this wasn't the first old car she'd owned. "And every single bit's expensive. Mind you . . ." She was feeling slightly smug, because she'd replaced the windscreen wipers herself, which had to be a saving.

She told him about her cleverness, and he listened admiringly.

"That deserves a drink," he'd said, and she'd agreed.

It wasn't anyone's fault that the first pub he'd suggested had been closed for renovation, or that the one she'd tried had had a large, noisy office party in, or that the third one had looked like a scene from a horror film.

There again, the park bench hadn't been that uncomfortable, and the warm cans of cola had tasted pretty good to a throat parched by a combination of nerves and heat.

"So what do you give up when you have to pay for car repairs?" he'd asked, which was an unusual chat-up line.

"Eating out; eating at all, come to that. Still, it'll do me good."

"Nonsense. You don't need to lose weight."

Not only had he said that flatteringly promptly, he'd managed to sound sincere; which meant he was either a dangerous conman, or every bit as nice as he seemed.

Helen remembered where he worked. She decided not to make her mind up just yet, but gave him the benefit of the doubt.

"You're sweet, but you need your eyes testing if you believe that. I ought to take up jogging."

"Me, too."

He'd looked at a stomach that, whilst not actually straining the waistband of his trousers, was definitely there.

"We could go together!"

Which they had, till he'd been knocked flying by a speeding in-line skater. Then she'd taken him to Casualty and sat with him for hours till they pronounced his ankle badly strained. That had been the end of their get-fit plans — but not the end of their relationship.

Helen had driven him home and made him dinner. Then they'd watched TV. If they'd happened to kiss as they'd snuggled on the settee that had been their business and no-one else's, and it had been an enormous relief when the seat didn't give way!

AND now here they were, stuck in the middle of the lake. Simon was bailing as fast as he could, but there was more water in the bottom of the boat with every second.

"Are you sure I shouldn't be rowing for shore?" she asked nervously.

"I'm not sure of anything," he snapped, which was a first. Then he made the effort to grin. "Unless you can remember the theme tune from 'Titanic'?"

She considered this, then shook her head.

"I think," he sloshed one last cupful over the side, then reached for the oars, "you're right. If we're lucky, we should just make it before it sinks."

"You think we're going to be lucky?" she shot back, then wished she hadn't because Simon just looked at her. It wasn't his normal joky look, nor the tender one he sometimes wore, but a blank look, as if she'd hurt his feelings.

"Do you?" he asked, slicing the oars through the water as if attacking his worst enemy. "We haven't done well so far, have we? Why should we think we've got a chance? And I tried so hard; today was meant to be perfect."

"It was." She took an oar from him and put her back into it, because they were, quite literally, in the same boat.

"Which is why you're up to your ankles in water," he said gloomily.

"So are you," Helen pointed out. "And anyway, you couldn't have known we'd picked the one leaky boat."

"I picked it," he corrected her gloomily. "Because I liked the name."

"What is its name?" She'd been too busy getting ants out of her shoes at the time.

"You mean you didn't look? Well, I guess I shouldn't be surprised," he said crossly.

"Simon." She stopped rowing, because she didn't think her feet couldn't get any wetter than they were. Even if they could, this mattered more.

"I've had a great time with you. I always do, and if things go wrong, well, you always get 'A' for effort."

"And 'E' for achievement." He only said what she'd been thinking earlier, but it was the last straw.

"That's not fair on yourself. Think of all the laughs we've had, and . . ." She took a deep breath. "And I've enjoyed every minute."

She'd had more polished boyfriends, but none like Simon, and it was Simon that she'd just realised that she loved.

"Really?" His smile was like the sun coming out. "Me, too, but we'd better get rowing. I'm going to give the owner a piece of my mind."

Helen, normally the most placid of girls, agreed with that by the time they got to shore. She was wet, but at least they were in one piece, so she let him go ahead of her because there was something she wanted to see.

It took a lot of tugging to get the boat out of the water now it was waterlogged, but she managed it, and saw the name, painted in fading, swirly letters.

"Oh!" She gasped and sank down on to the grass. She was still sitting there when he came back.

"What's up?" he asked worriedly, and she tried to smile.

"I saw the boat's name, and I've put my back out!"

"Oh, Helen." He didn't say anything else. He didn't need to, because they both knew that the boat's name had been the right one.

As he picked her up and carried her to the car, ignoring her protests that she could manage, she knew the day deserved "A" for achievement as well as effort.

Just like the boat, this had to be True Love. ❏

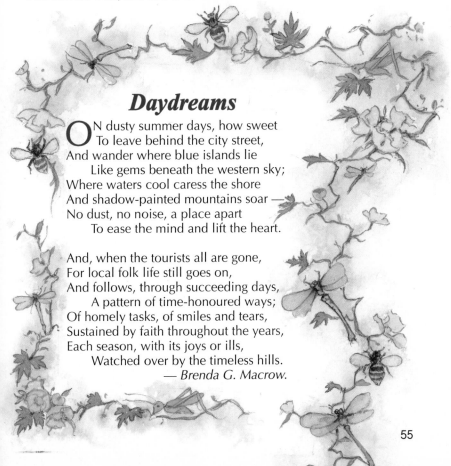

Daydreams

ON dusty summer days, how sweet
    To leave behind the city street,
And wander where blue islands lie
    Like gems beneath the western sky;
Where waters cool caress the shore
And shadow-painted mountains soar —
No dust, no noise, a place apart
    To ease the mind and lift the heart.

And, when the tourists all are gone,
For local folk life still goes on,
And follows, through succeeding days,
    A pattern of time-honoured ways;
Of homely tasks, of smiles and tears,
Sustained by faith throughout the years,
Each season, with its joys or ills,
    Watched over by the timeless hills.
              — *Brenda G. Macrow.*

A UNT PENNY was a fanatical gardener. So I ought to have known that when I invited her over to show off my new home, she would display only a polite interest in the size of rooms, the potential in the attic, and the breadth of the hall.

Instead, her eyes were riveted assessingly on the ground between the gate and the front door — and the generous stretch of weeds at the back.

"Perfect," she breathed.

I tried to deflect her over lunch, enlarging on my plans for the decorating, the furnishings and the kitchen, but all I got was, "Very nice, dear." Aunt Penny's mind was on other things.

At twenty-five, I appreciated that I was privileged to have my

Illustration by Gerard Fay.

How Does Yo

wn place. And I'd be the first to acknowledge that it hadn't been all my own work.

I *had* saved hard where I could. I'd gone without a car and holidays, but upon my dear parents by living at ome . . . They'd let me pay for my keep for my own pride's sake, but had flatly refused anything more. The bank account had mounted.

I hadn't realised Uncle Matthew had been keeping tabs on me. A successful businessman and a bachelor, he'd been watching my financial habits with approval.

One day at Sunday lunch, the conversation had been filled with his enthusiasm about home-ownership. Then he'd turned to me.

"Time to be investing in your own place, Tilly," he'd said. "How much have you saved?"

I was startled, but I told him, wondering if I'd get praise or censure.

Uncle Matt leaned an elbow on the table.

"Well done, my dear," he said. "Very well done, indeed."

He stretched back in his chair with the utmost satisfaction. "You've done so much for yourself that I feel you've earned a helping hand."

By the end of the meal, dazed but delighted, I realised that I could go out and find a place to buy, and that he would put down the rest of the money.

I could pay off the mortgage to him. I couldn't believe my ears.

Within six months, I was the proud owner of a two-bedroomed cottage sitting in its own wilderness.

* * * *

Enter Aunt Penny. She's Uncle Matt's sister and still suffers from sibling rivalry. Maybe that prompted her suggestion, although I liked to think it was her affection for me.

We sat outside in the sunshine, sipping tea.

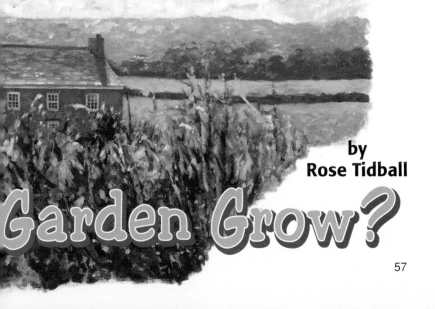

by
Rose Tidball

Garden Grow?

57

"What," she enquired, "do you intend to do with the garden?"

I looked round vaguely. It's funny how people all have different priorities.

"Why?" I said. "What's wrong with it? It makes a super bird sanctuary."

"Mm," she said. "Nature's all very well. But perfection comes when we work together."

"I don't know anything about gardening," I muttered defensively.

"It'll grow on you," Aunt Penny said cheerfully, unaware of her pun. "All you need is a hand with this jungle. I know the very chap — landscape gardener."

"Oh, Aunt Penny!" I sighed. "I've got my work cut out with all the things there are to do in the house . . . I can't afford to have someone in. Can't I just cut the worst back and leave it till I can afford to do something about it?"

"Nonsense." Aunt Penny looked, for a moment, exactly like her brother. "Gardens take time to get going. The sooner you tackle it, the better.

"Anyway, I was thinking of giving you the garden as a house-warming present. It won't cost you a thing. And I promise you'll love what this chap will do."

What could I say? I had the feeling that things were going quicker than I could cope with, but who was I to quarrel with this remarkable family of mine?

SO that was how it was that the van turned up one evening. *Russ Stafford, Landscape Gardener,* it said on the side. Aunt Penny had lost no time.

Russ Stafford came to the back door with a clipboard.

"Your aunt . . ." he began.

"I know," I said briefly. "Come in."

I made him some tea and we sat at the kitchen table. He didn't seem at all dismayed by the task before him, I have to say.

Then we walked as far as we could round the boundaries. That was difficult — I don't think anyone had touched the ground for forty years. The undergrowth was full of rubbish. But Russ wasn't pessimistic. He kicked a hummock, and smiled at the dark earth that was exposed.

"Loam," he murmured. "It's been a cottage garden for a couple of centuries at least. They dug in all their ash and compost."

"I wouldn't know where to start," I confessed, looking around.

"There's nothing worth keeping, which can be a good thing. It means you can start from scratch. Let's make a list of your favourite plants."

We went indoors again.

"Now then!" He regarded me with calm and kindly hazel eyes.

Russ was a big man, long in the arm and leg. He looked incredibly healthy. That was because of all the work he did outdoors, I supposed. In my job in a lawyers' office, I was used to men who spent their lives in the office or in their cars.

I realised I was staring and blushed. But he had got up again, and was standing by the window looking down the back garden.

"Right. Let's hear your plant preference!"

"Uhhh." I grabbed at thin air. "Scented things. Winter flowers. And . . ." I remembered Aunt Penny's garden and a spectacular spring tree where purple, pea-like flowers grew directly from the trunk, up every branch . . .

"A Judas tree," I finished triumphantly, and he nodded.

"Well, you're sheltered, with all-day sun, and we're not far from the coast. Should be OK."

"It'll have to be low maintenance," I told him. "I haven't much time."

"Your aunt's arranged all that with me," he murmured.

* * * *

Russ began work the following week. On Monday night I returned home to a bramble-free front path. He'd taken off all the top growth, and a huge pile of gleanings had been left to dry at the foot of the garden.

Then he rang me.

"Do you mind if I come over on Saturday?" he asked. "It's just that we're well into October, the weather's holding fine and it would be as well to crack on while conditions are good. Once the rains set in, we could be soggy until February."

I told him it would be OK. For some reason, I found myself shopping for a casserole dish and a thick pair of working gloves. Perhaps it was time I took an interest in this gardening lark . . .

He arrived early with a power-fork, two sets of secateurs, a saw, and a strange implement with a cross-blade that he used for cutting through roots.

"I could take all the rubbish away, but I thought we could have a bonfire. That would destroy the seeds on the surface, sweeten the ground and give us potash. Nothing wasted."

I'd changed into old jeans and a worn-out sweater by that time, and he seemed to relish the company. We were soon working as a team. Russ cut up the clods and freed the roots, and wheeled it round to the bonfire, which sent up a reassuring plume.

I became very warm and smelled strongly of bonfire. This was much better than an hour on those machines down at the gym!

Of course, we had to stop for tea and coffee on the hour, and we talked.

His elder brother ran the family farm, so Russ had branched out on his own with several acres of land and some glasshouses.

"I'm contracted out most of the summer," he explained. "Like builders, everyone wants you then. There's not a lot to be done over December and January, so that's when I can catch up on my own stuff and have a bit of time off if I feel like it."

"Does your brother give you a hand?" I asked.

"I usually end up helping Ralph! Oh, we help each other, but the farm won't support us all, and he's the one with the family.

"It's funny, but when the land's been in your blood for centuries, you find it difficult to move into other things. I'm lucky things have turned out as they have . . ."

At lunchtime I asked him in for the casserole and a baked potato. It was wonderful to watch him eat. I'd never realised how many people were faddy eaters! It was wonderful to see Russ clear his plate with evident enjoyment.

I bet he likes steamed golden syrup sponge, I thought, making a mental note for next Saturday.

I told him about my job, made him laugh with little stories of my family, and talked a lot about Aunt Penny, whom he liked.

Apparently she'd asked him over to give her a hand one spring after she'd had flu, and from then on she'd recommended him to all her friends.

"Got me started." He grinned. "She's quite a lady, and she has a wonderful way with plants.

"I put so much work into raising them, but some people don't give them any attention at all after they've bought them! I don't worry when your aunt carries them off, though. They're going to a good home!"

Without knowing it, I was picking up lots of information about gardening. His sheer enthusiasm was infectious.

During November, it started to tip down. Work ground to a halt, and I missed Russ. We'd become good friends over the weeks — close even.

On my side, I had become aware of a current drawing me ever nearer to him. I looked forward to his visits, and woke up each morning with a sense of gladness, of anticipation.

There was only one snag. Although he obviously liked me, there was a reserve about him which I couldn't understand. Surely — we were both unattached — the time had come for him to ask me out. But that was the line he didn't seem to want to cross.

I didn't see him for most of December. But just before Christmas, he turned up with a card and a handsome flowering cactus.

Over coffee, he told me he was spending the holiday with his brother and family, and hoped the weather would cheer up soon so that we could get on with the garden.

When he'd gone, I looked out of the window at the cleared, brown, barren earth. My heart was beginning to feel wintry, too.

Just after New Year, Aunt Penny turned up.

"It's wonderful!" she exclaimed. How could anyone get so enthusiastic about a sea of mud?

"And all that can become, within weeks, a riot of colour and vitality . . ." she went on. "You'd never believe it, looking at it now."

I joined her, and tried to agree. Aunt Penny gave me a swift look.

"Nice chap, isn't he?" she murmured absently.

When I didn't answer, she went on.

"Shame about the way he was treated."

I looked at her questioningly.

"I've known Sheila Vanscombe since she was a child," she mused. "Flighty sort of girl. But he fell for her, of course. She had a way with her.

"And he was an innocent . . . you can imagine it, shut away on the farm, meeting few people, working all the time. When he fell for Sheila, he began to make plans . . . If you ask me, it was a blessing that she left."

"What happened?" I asked, my heart beating faster.

"Oh, she went off with some chap she met at the yacht club. That was the sort of life which really suited her. She wouldn't have done for Russ at all.

"But it struck him badly. He began working twice as hard, really got his head down. It's done something to his confidence if you ask me. He is, after all, a shy man."

Shy! That explained a lot. I remembered so many little signs . . .

Aunt Penny was watching me, wry sympathy in her eyes.

"Give him time, my dear," she said.

FEBRUARY burst upon us with night frosts and brilliant, bright days. People didn't walk down the road, they waltzed. Spring, we all told one another, was on its way. A thrush began a tentative warble down the road, catkins smothered a hazel tree, and Russ rang.

"I just wanted to see you about the lay-out," he said. "Can I call on Saturday?"

My heart burst into blossom as well. The sun shone into the cottage and prompted me to extra polishing and burnishing. I even made a cake.

Although I hadn't seen him for a few weeks, the familiar figure coming up the path filled me with joy. I longed to put my arms around him.

Instead, I smiled a welcome, made him coffee, sat him by the fire and feigned enthusiasm for his plans.

"A terrace from the back door, then three steps down. Crazy-paving path leading you on to a little winter copse, with witch-hazels — you can get them in three colours now — and a viburnum and a daphne, which will give you scent and flowers.

"I thought we could get a mahonia in here. You remember, the greeny-yellow flowers which smell of lily of the valley and bloom all winter?"

"It sounds great."

He seemed pleased.

"Then your Judas tree can make a statement here, in the lawn. Its purple flowers will be great against the grass.

"And I wondered . . ." He gave me a quick, uncertain glance. "I didn't want to make too much work for you, but I thought — one small bed? It would give you the chance to ring the changes every season as the fancy took you . . . You could pot up with stocks, or hyacinths, or . . . anything?"

I nodded, and he rolled up the plan.

"That's settled, then. I can make a start. All this stuff is pot-grown, so there's no difficulty in getting it in."

"Next Saturday?"

He hesitated.

"I was thinking of Monday, as the forecast is so good. Is that OK?"

I nodded, disappointed. I would be at work.

*　*　*　*

"Come on, Tilly! You must have got *one.*"

My friends were giggling over their Valentines. Though I did my best to respond to the fun, I was feeling ridiculously forlorn.

I'd sent Russ a card, anonymously, but all the postman had left me was junk mail and a postcard from two friends who were on honeymoon.

It had become milder. But the sunshine still warmed bare twigs. I drove home in the winter dusk. The mere thought of Russ working at the cottage that day lifted my spirits, though. I put my car away, feeling his presence all round the place.

As I walked down the path, I could see the infant shrubs which he'd planted. I went round the back.

He'd finished the terrace some days ago, and the transformation was amazing, even in that uncertain light. He'd obviously managed to get the turf in today . . . I walked down the crazy-paving path, and there it was. His Valentine!

He'd cut a heart-shaped bed out of the grass. It was edged with red polyanthus, and filled with . . .

I rushed back into the cottage and got a torch. The bed was filled with dwarf red tulips, their leaves striped, blooming bravely in the winter night.

I stared until the night air chilled me. Then, my heart full, my head hammering, I rushed back to my car and drove quickly through the lanes.

There was a light on in his cottage.

When he opened the door I rushed into his arms, hardly able to speak with joy.

"I thought you'd like it," he said, kissing me.

And he's been kissing me ever since! ❏

by Mikala Pope

W HEN I was Duncan's age we had to make our own amusement."
Alistair Grantley frowned.

"But things have changed, Dad," June pointed out.

"And not for the better! On a lovely afternoon like this, we'd be out playing football, or down the park with a fishing net, catching tadpoles, not stuck in front of a computer all day."

"But he was playing outside all morning."

LIKE FATHER, LIKE SON

"If you ask me, you spoil that boy." Alistair folded his newspaper, then got up stiffly from the armchair.

"I'm going to my room. Don't bother to bring me a cup of tea. I'll make my own. It's just as well I brought my electric kettle with me. It's one little thing I can do for myself, without burdening others."

"But, Dad . . ."

Without another word, he picked up his paper and left the room.

* * * *

"Darling, whatever's the matter?" Derek asked when he came in.

"Nothing's the matter," June insisted.

"But you've been crying."

"It's these onions."

Derek gently kissed his wife's red-rimmed eyes.

"Come on, something's wrong, isn't it? Is it Dad?"

"I know I shouldn't get upset, but he always seems to be finding fault with Duncan."

"What was it this time?" Derek sighed.

"Something and nothing, really. He reckons Duncan's spending too

63

much time on his computer when he should be out in the fresh air. It's not as though we let him spend hours using it, is it? And he was playing outside with his friends all morning."

"I'll have a quiet word with Dad later."

"No, don't do that. He'll only think I've been grumbling about him. He said this afternoon something about being a burden to us. You know I never think that, don't you?"

"Of course I do," Derek assured her.

"I think the world of your dad. It's just that, when I'm feeling a bit tired, and he goes on about how we're bringing up Duncan, well . . . sometimes, I let it get on top of me, I suppose."

"I do hope we've made the right decision, asking him to move in."

June saw the look of concern spread over her husband's face.

"Of course we have! He just wasn't coping on his own, and for most of the time he's a poppet. It's early days yet, and there are bound to be a few teething troubles." June kissed her husband. "Now, don't hold up the cook! It's steak and kidney pudding tonight — Dad's favourite."

Their ten-year-old son came bounding into the kitchen.

"Mum! Is it all right if Andy comes round to play in the morning?" Duncan asked.

"Of course! Now go and wash your hands, it's almost time for supper."

"I'm starving! What is it?"

"Good old steak and kidney pud," his dad replied.

Duncan's face fell.

"Oh, Mum! It's Friday! Why don't we ever have Chinese take-aways on Fridays now?"

"Grandad doesn't like Chinese food," his mother replied.

A LISTAIR GRANTLEY found the battered old suitcase in the wardrobe and took it over to his armchair by the window. The sun was streaming into the room and felt pleasantly warm against his back. He opened the case and tipped its contents carefully on to the bed.

He'd had to get rid of so many things when he'd left the bungalow, but that was hardly surprising — forty years was a long time. Forty years! Who would have believed it? In many ways, it seemed like only yesterday that he'd met Mary.

He could still remember clearly how she'd looked that day, as she waited in the bus queue. It had just started to rain, and he'd plucked up the courage to ask her if she'd like to share his umbrella.

It had been the first really warm day of spring and he could even remember the summer dress she was wearing. She had looked so pretty — no, that was the wrong word — she had looked beautiful, as beautiful as she still was when they celebrated their ruby wedding last July.

Derek and June had completely cleared out their spare room for him, so he'd been able to bring some things from the bungalow. He knew it was silly, keeping Mary's piano, when he couldn't play a note. But it had meant so much to her and he couldn't bear the thought of it being carted off to the auction with the rest of the furniture.

Although not a word was spoken, he knew that they understood.

From the pile on the bed, he took a bundle tied in pink ribbon — Christmas, birthday and anniversary cards going back over the years. There were some things from which he would never be parted.

He would just look through the cards for now. He would save the rest for other days; the letters they'd sent to each other before they were married; the theatre programmes they'd kept; Derek's old school reports; the photographs; even the bus tickets from that first journey they'd made together; and so many other things that would mean nothing to anyone else, but that to him and Mary were precious beyond price.

Come to think of it, the piano had really been bought for Derek, hadn't it? How old would he have been? Ten, perhaps? About the same age as Duncan was now. Of course, they hadn't really been able to afford a piano, but Mary had so wanted to share her love of music with Derek; a little bit of scrimping and saving and they had managed it.

He took a card from the pile on the bed — the one he had sent to Mary on their very first anniversary. It looked rather old-fashioned now. How young they had been then, and so much in love. It was a love that grew and deepened as the years went by.

And what was this? A piece of white card, folded neatly in half, with a carefully crayoned-in drawing of a policeman on the front.

He opened it and read, *Happy Christmas to Mummy and Daddy with love from Derek.* Mary had written underneath, *From our darling Derek, aged five.* He looked at the front again. No, it couldn't be a policeman! It must be Father Christmas . . . or was it a snowman?

Like his dad, Derek wasn't much of an artist, but he did share his mother's love of music. Alistair closed his eyes. He could see his young son sitting next to Mary on the piano stool, and in his mind he could hear them playing together again.

He smiled to himself as he remembered how hard Derek had tried to teach him to play "Chopsticks", only to despair at his father's inability to make it sound anything like the tune.

He took another card from the pile. This time the figure on the front had been neatly coloured with felt-tip pens rather than crayons, though he still couldn't make out whether Derek had intended it to be Father Christmas or a snowman.

However, when he opened it, he discovered that it wasn't from Derek. *Happy Christmas to Granny and Grandad with love from Duncan.* Mary had written underneath, *From our dear Duncan, aged six.*

He couldn't quite understand why, but as he put the two cards together and saw how alike they were, tears filled his eyes.

Alistair got up from his chair and walked across the room to the piano, lifted the lid, and ran his fingers lightly over the keys. He would never know what it was that brought back a memory so long forgotten, but it was as though he could hear his own father speaking the words again.

"Derek should be outside with his friends rather than banging away on that thing all the time. Spending all that money on a piano, too! It's nothing to do with me, but I'm afraid you're spoiling that boy."

Alistair had been cross with his father, but immediately regretted it. Dad hadn't meant his words to be hurtful — but hurtful they'd been. And now, only this afternoon, he had hurt June in much the same way. There was truth in that old saying, "Like father, like son".

He went back to his chair and took another card — not from the bundle, but from the wallet inside his jacket pocket where he always kept it. How Mary had remembered that it was his birthday, he would never know — she had been so very poorly.

She must have asked one of the nurses to buy it for her — probably that nice young girl who was always so kind.

She'd been so weak that it must have taken such a long time to write. The words were very unsteady but every letter was written with love.

He shouldn't have got cross with his father like that, but he'd been so hurt by the older man's harsh words. Of course, Mary had put everything right between them, and never again had there been any problems. He never found out exactly what she'd said to his father, but before long, he, too, had been trying his hand at playing "Chopsticks" with his grandson.

Of one thing Alistair was certain — whatever words Mary had spoken to his father, they would have been said with the same love as had guided her hand when she wrote that last card.

He heard June calling to Duncan that supper was ready. If only Mary was here now. She would know how a foolish old man, who sometimes spoke without thinking, could put everything right again.

The slight feeling of unease that had been present after the upset of

Muckross Lake, Killarney

THE Killarney Lakeland is a spectacular area, with its mild climate and rapid changes in light. The National Park here includes some 25,000 acres of dense woodland and three major lakes, including Muckross, also known as Middle Lake.

In the 18th century, the local gentry would hunt around the lake's surrounding woodland. On reaching the water, the chase would continue in boats.

Nearby lies the centrepiece of this beautiful area, 19th century Muckross House, with its lovely gardens and some 65 rooms. Now a museum, the mansion is home to craftsmen — potters, blacksmiths and weavers — who can be seen working at their age-old trades.

MUCKROSS LAKE, KILLARNEY: J CAMPBELL KERR

The People's Friend Annual

the afternoon soon disappeared as Duncan chatted away about his plans to play with Andy the next day.

"Any more steak and kidney pudding, Dad?" Derek offered.

Alistair pushed his plate to the side.

"I'd like to, but I'd burst. That was delicious. You can't beat a good old-fashioned steak and kidney pud."

"Now, who's for fruit salad?" June asked.

"Me, please!" Duncan responded enthusiastically.

Derek cleared the plates from the table, while his wife brought in the bowl of fruit salad.

"So, if your friend's coming to play tomorrow, you won't be using your computer, will you?" Duncan's grandad asked him.

JUNE and Derek exchanged an anxious glance. Oh, dear! If Dad was about to deliver another lecture, how should they respond? Quite unaware of the tension that his parents were feeling, Duncan's reply was spontaneous.

"I might, when Andy's gone."

His mum and dad waited anxiously.

"Then, do you think you could show me how to use it?"

"Of course!" Duncan replied, as though it was the most natural request in the world.

"You! Use the computer?" Derek blurted out in surprise.

"Don't sound so shocked!" Alistair chuckled. "I'm not quite in my dotage, yet, you know."

"No, I didn't mean that." Derek laughed. "But, I didn't think you were interested in Duncan's computer."

"I had a letter from your Aunt Dorothy in Canada the other week. She said something about getting in touch with her by . . . what's it called?"

"E-mail?" Duncan helped his grandad out.

"That's it! Can you do that on your computer?"

"Of course I can! It's dead easy! I'll show you after supper, if you like."

"Talking about supper — tonight I've had my favourite steak and kidney pud, so tomorrow I think it should be Duncan's turn. I'd like to treat you all to a Chinese take-away, if that's all right, June." Alistair glanced at his daughter-in-law.

"Smashing!" Duncan whooped.

"That's very kind of you, Dad, but you don't like Chinese food, do you?" June said gently.

"To be honest, I've never tried it, but it's high time that I did."

"And can I use chopsticks again, Mum?" Duncan asked.

"As long as you don't expect me to." June laughed.

"Will you try chopsticks, Grandad?"

"If you teach me how," Alistair replied with a smile, as in his heart he said a little word of thanks to Mary. ❏

68

Illustration
by Melvyn
Warren-Smith.

Mrs Amos's Big Day

HETTY AMOS loved weddings. She always had. As a child,
she'd longed to be a bridesmaid but, alas, no bride had
ever asked her.

She knew she was no beauty, of course, but she was
absolutely certain that she'd be instantly transformed into a princess
if only she could wear one of those rustling pink dresses and a
twinkling silver headband.

Oh, the hours she'd spent outside church railings, peering

by Valerie Edwards

through the narrow gap. She'd held her breath when the bride appeared in her flowing white gown, veil flung back, walking straight and proud by her brand new husband's side. Not that Hetty ever paid much attention to the groom. But she looked on the bridesmaids with envy and sighed — a deep, heavy sigh.

And then, just as she was about to turn away, she'd feel the hand on her shoulder.

"You'll be the death of me, our Hetty," her mother would say, steering the little girl ahead of her as they marched up the street. Mum had usually been shopping and the bag would bang painfully against the back of Hetty's knees.

"I always know where to find you, come four o'clock on a Saturday."

"Oh, she was lovely, Mum," Hetty would breathe.

"Yes, well, why don't you wait for your own big day," her mother would say, her voice softening. "Save it all up till then."

But, in the event, there wasn't one. Not a proper church wedding, at any rate, with a special dress and a sit-down meal.

Instead, she'd had to make do with a registry office and a weekend honeymoon at a B & B in Ilfracombe. Bill had been in the Army and that was all the leave he'd had owing. And then he was off to Cyprus.

He'd been her first boyfriend and she'd been scared of losing him, thinking about all those better-looking girls he'd be bound to meet overseas.

"I should grab him while you can, our Hetty," her mother had warned her gloomily.

So it had been a special licence and Hetty had minded terribly but she hadn't let on. Bill hadn't wanted a church wedding anyway.

"All show," he'd said. "A waste of money."

At least she'd wanted a nice frock or suit — something special to mark the occasion — but, in the end, there hadn't been enough time, or enough money.

IN the years that followed, Bill never found out about her surreptitious visits on Saturday afternoons. He was always out himself, at the football or the cricket.

He thought she went shopping. And she did, in a way. Shopping for pleasure.

They'd jogged along like most married couples for thirty-five years, until she got home one Saturday afternoon and found a policeman on the doorstep.

Bill had died in the closing minutes of a football match, just as the home team had scored the equalising goal. A heart attack, it had been — from the excitement, they thought. That was a few winters ago.

Now, it was Saturday afternoon yet again. She'd tried working it out only last night, but couldn't remember exactly how many brides she'd seen over the years. She thought it must be hundreds.

She'd always tried to look her best, even though she'd only ever been an onlooker.

Except that once, just over a year ago, she'd actually been mistaken for a guest. A proper, invited guest.

She'd worn her new two-piece suit and the silver earrings Bill had given her for their twenty-fifth anniversary.

She'd looked out at the cloudless blue sky and decided not to take an umbrella. The weather forecast had predicted another fine day. She shut the front door behind her and stood for a moment breathing in the warm, sultry air. Then she headed off down the street, smiling happily to herself.

Most of the guests had taken their seats by the time she arrived, but as she stood at the railings, she saw a few stragglers still turning up.

She sighed, as she always did, at some of the clothes the younger ones thought appropriate these days.

SUDDENLY, she felt the first drops of rain on her face. Then the heavens opened, and it poured down. Within seconds, a streak of lightning flashed across the sky and an ominous rumble of thunder came hard on its heels.

Hetty had a great fear of thunderstorms, inherited from her mother, who'd shut the two of them in the cupboard under the stairs whenever one was imminent.

She took a few steps forward, and then, as an even louder thunderclap rent the air, she took to her heels and ran.

Surely no-one would mind, she thought breathlessly, as she reached the heavy oak door of the church. If she stayed outside, she'd get drenched.

She crept inside and quickly sank into the back row. No head turned. She heaved a sigh of relief.

Then she was aware of a touch at her elbow and an open prayer book was proffered. She glanced up. A man smiled down at her, then indicated a line in the book. She nodded her thanks.

When the congregation got to their feet, she rose also and joined in "Holy Holy Holy", a remembered childhood favourite. She was aware of her neighbour's deep, pleasant baritone, and her own rather piping soprano.

Mrs Amos relaxed, beginning to enjoy herself.

She was sorry when the wedding party moved to the vestry to sign the register. Soon after their triumphal procession down the aisle, she prepared to leave herself.

"Oh, no, it's still raining!" she said aloud, dismayed. Photographs were abandoned as guests streamed past, most at the gallop.

"Come on," her neighbour said, propelling her forward. "My car's just over here. I'll give you a lift to the reception."

"No," she began. "No, you don't understand. It was just this awful weather . . ."

The wind whipped the words from her lips and she almost slipped on the wet grass.

"Here," he said cheerfully. He pulled open the car door. "There you go." He ran round to the driver's seat and leapt in. He switched on the ignition, then pulled away from the kerb. Mrs Amos fell silent, trying to think of words, embarrassed beyond measure.

"I nearly didn't come," he said. "I mean, on my own. It's always a bit awkward at these kind of things. And I'm actually only a distant cousin. It was nice of them to remember me."

"Yes," Mrs Amos said faintly.

"So you can see I'm more than glad of your company. If you don't mind," he added anxiously.

He's shy, she thought, with sudden insight. Poor chap. I know just how he feels. But she had to tell him.

"Look, I shouldn't be here," she started, but he was intent now on manoeuvring the medium-sized car into a minuscule parking space.

They got out. People jostled them into the entrance and they passed the line of the smiling bridal party at speed. Mrs Amos could hardly catch the greetings in the general hubbub.

There was a buffet, and it was crowded. He guided her, with a solicitous hand at her elbow, to a place in a corner where she leaned thankfully — and guiltily — against the cool wall.

He was back within minutes, a full plate balanced precariously in either hand. She realised she was actually hungry, but she averted her gaze, telling herself firmly that it was now or never.

"I'm here under false pretences," she announced in a loud voice. It still seemed to come out as a squeak. She tried again.

"Sorry," she added lamely. "I did try and tell you. I just went into the church to get out of the rain."

He stared at her, a minute sausage roll halfway to his mouth. Then, unbelievably, he laughed. After a second or two, she found herself reluctantly joining in.

"It's true," she insisted. "I just love weddings, seeing the bride in all her glory. And it's the first time anything like this has ever happened to me. Honestly."

"Oh, I believe you," he said. He wiped his eyes, the amusement still vivid in his face.

"No-one could make it up. But, look, I shan't let on if you don't. I'm enjoying myself too much. I hope you are."

"I am," she agreed fervently.

"Then tuck in," he invited. "The food's delicious."

Afterwards, he'd driven her home and she'd asked him in for a coffee. They'd talked for ages, but later, thinking about it, she couldn't remember what the conversation had been about. But she realised she felt young again, tremulous with anticipation. And the marvellous thing was, she knew he felt the same.

Now, she began to dress.

The pale silk slid over her head and fell to her knees. She smoothed it over her hips, glad she'd not put on any surplus pounds in all these years. Then she fixed the flowers in her hair and examined herself in the mirror.

The smile lifted the corners of her lips. She felt like a little girl once more, looking through the railings, agog with excitement, as she waited for the lucky bride. Only, this time, it was different.

She stood up as the knock came at the door and then hurried to answer it.

"Taxi for the bride," the driver said, touching his cap.

"I'm ready," she said.

She picked up her bouquet and almost skipped down the path to the waiting car.

Mrs Amos's Big Day had arrived at last. And she was determined not to miss a single second of it. ❏

The Prime of Miss Jean Brodie

FILMED entirely on location in 1969, from the novel by Muriel Spark, "The Prime of Miss Jean Brodie" earned its star, Maggie Smith, an Academy Award.

Thirties' Edinburgh is beautifully conjured up by clever use of the city's historical streets and buildings. The school at which Miss Brodie instructs her girls, the Marcia Blaine School for Girls, was recreated in Donaldson's School for the Deaf.

Greyfriars Churchyard provided the setting for a lengthy sermon from Miss Brodie. The churchyard is steeped in Scottish history — though most people tend to associate it with Greyfriars Bobby, the famously loyal Skye terrier.

Another grand location used by the film-makers was mediaeval Barnbougle Castle, situated just outside Edinburgh. Strangely, it was used as the home for Mr Lowther, played by Gordon Jackson — a rather impressive property for a humble teacher!

On The Silver Screen

73

Illustration by Anita Våmartveit.

L IKE the shimmering sea, the sky was a perfect blue. The sun was a glowing golden orb, and not a suggestion of a breeze disturbed the leafy trees.

It was a tranquil early summer day — the kind to sit back and appreciate the precious gifts from Mother Nature and calmly take stock of life . . .

74

A Holiday Romance

by Patti Hales

But that wasn't exactly the mood inside my elderly car, where my sister, Faye, was leaping up and down, making the suspension creak alarmingly.

"I wasn't expecting any excitement, Erin. I didn't think there'd be any at wherever-we-are-on-sea. Only fabulous scenery, silvery sands, and a quaint village within walking distance — wasn't that what the blurb in the brochure promised? Well, it seems they were wrong."

I smiled fondly. All I cared about was that we were on holiday!

Faye widened her eyes dramatically.

"Look at him! He is, without doubt, destiny's dream man. I think I'm in love." Faye barely paused for breath as we pulled up outside caravan number 17.

I hid a smile. Faye's wonderfully impetuous. Gloriously optimistic — and utterly drop-dead gorgeous!

75

She has a glamorous career, whereas mine is just the opposite. We're probably the most unidentical twins in the history of womankind.

If I didn't love Faye, I would envy her. But I do love her. There isn't a nasty bone in her slim, perfect body. She's my best, most supportive friend in the world, constantly trying to bolster my self-confidence.

"There's my holiday romance organised already," she carried on, after fluffing up her blonde hair and fixing her big round eyes on the dark-haired, broad-shouldered hunk who was sprawled on a sun lounger just a few feet away.

Meanwhile, his companion — shorter, slighter, and with shorter, neater hair — staggered under the weight of an enormous cardboard box crammed with tinned food.

"Tall, dark and mind-blowingly handsome. What more could a girl ask for, Erin?" she finished, dreamily, checking her flawless cerise lipstick — which exactly matched her designer shorts and strappy top — in the driving mirror.

It was half an hour later before I got round to considering her question.

View of Arran, as seen from Kintyre.

Dennis Hardley.

BY then, cool as a cucumber, Faye was sprawled on the grass, her fake-tanned legs arranged for maximum effect, deep in conversation with the object of her desire, who was looking at her as though all his Christmases had come at once.

While plain, organised little me had already transferred most of our baggage from the car boot to the tiny combined living-room, bedroom and mini-kitchen under a fiercely burning sun.

I was all too uncomfortably aware that my long, straight mousey hair was damp with perspiration, that the flick of mascara I'd applied earlier was probably sliding down my cheeks. Lipstick? I hadn't bothered with that.

After all, no-one took much notice of me when Faye was around.

Unusually, I experienced a rare loss of sense of humour.

"A girl *could* ask for a bit of help," I called out, rather stroppily, to be honest, as I struggled and eventually admitted defeat with the heaviest suitcase.

Under A Blue Sky

THE mountains lean against the sky
All lapped in sunlit haze,
And lazily the seagulls fly,
Like paper kites that soar on high
On halcyon summer days.

A rough road makes the rambler long
For paths where waters meet —
The scent of myrtle, spicy-strong,
The murmur of a hill-burn's song
Beneath the trackless peat.

We see wild flowers of every hue
Along the stony miles.
High hills that dominate the view
And, growing out of distance blue,
The glory of the Isles!

Long, summer days of carefree ease,
So soon to disappear.
Relaxing under sun-warmed trees,
We gather precious memories
To last us through the year!
                                — *Brenda G. Macrow.*

Faye's suitcase!

Witnessing me losing the battle, she immediately sprang to her feet, looking guilty — beautifully so, of course.

"Oh, sorry, Erin. I was just telling Nathan — this is Nathan, by the way, Nathan Bond — and he's here with his . . ."

"Let me," a soft, deep voice murmured in my ear.

"Josh," he introduced himself over a freckled shoulder, lifting the case as though it weighed next to nothing.

"Erin," I responded, equally economically.

"Thank you," I went on, as he disappeared through the narrow doorway of our temporary home.

It was only when Josh returned and flashed me a shy smile — filled with understanding and something else, which I couldn't quite fathom — that I realised that never, in my twenty-three years, had I looked into a pair of dark eyes quite as gentle and kind as these ones were . . .

IT wasn't the peak holiday season, because the schools hadn't yet broken up, so the caravan site was inhabited mostly by lovely elderly people who enjoyed evenings of Forties and Fifties music and the dances that went with the sounds.

So it was inevitable really, that the four of us — Nathan and Josh, Faye and myself — got together.

We went everywhere as a foursome, sharing picnics on the almost-deserted beach, enjoying long country walks, strolling into the village in the evening for the occasional meal at the one and only pub.

The sun continued to shine. There was lots of laughter, and loads of conversation. We were frequently amazed at just how *many* things we had in common.

But in spite of them looking like the kind of ideal glossy couple you usually only see in Hollywood films or newspaper gossip columns, Faye and Nathan seemed to get no further than being just friends.

That baffled me.

Nathan was a company director, and Josh an illustrator. Nathan explained that they had decided to come on this holiday because, although they used to be very close, they hadn't spent much time together lately.

In spite of his dashing looks, he was a down-to-earth fellow, with a terrific sense of humour and a sharp mind.

He was, in fact, exactly the kind of man my sister had always said would be the one to sweep her off her high-heeled feet. Beauty *and* brains!

I began to wonder if I'd missed something — a tell-tale glance between the couple, perhaps, or a long lingering kiss behind one of the tall briar hedges we frequently encountered on our long treks . . .

Eventually, I could stand the suspense no longer.

"Madly in love with Nathan yet, Faye?" I queried halfway through the week, trying to keep my tone nice and light.

She was re-varnishing her perfect fingernails an attractive coral colour, which even a non-cosmetic girl like myself knew would flatter her now-genuine golden tan.

Looking up, she calmly met my enquiring gaze.

"No, we're just mates. Still getting to know each other. Who knows . . .?"

Her smile turned a little mischievous.

"How about you, Erin? Getting any little romantic flutterings over our artist? He *is* talented, isn't he? That sketch he did of you is amazing."

Not being very good at fibbing, I could feel my cheeks grow hot. They'd done exactly the same when Josh had given me the drawing, which revealed a side of me I'd never seen before. Almost pretty, I'd secretly thought.

I'd gone the same shade of crimson when, earlier that day, Josh had gently taken my hand and helped me across the slippery stepping stones that were dotted haphazardly across a fast-running silver stream.

"It's OK, Erin. Come on. I'm here for you. I won't let you slip," he had promised, when my legs had gone so wobbly, halfway across, that I'd stood there, like a complete idiot, frozen to the mossy surface.

His eyes had looked deeply into mine and, just for a moment, I'd felt as though I could have flown across the stretch of bubbling water, right into his waiting arms . . .

"Don't be ridiculous," I told Faye, forcing what I'd hoped was a wry smile. "I'm not looking for Mr Right and, even if I was, Josh wouldn't be remotely interested in someone as ordinary as me.

"He's used to painting scenes of great beauty, remember. I'm hardly Mona Lisa, am I?"

With her small pink tongue protruding slightly, my twin, who *was* a scene of great beauty, shrugged, bent her glossy head and began meticulously painting the nails on her left hand.

"Who knows . . .?" she murmured.

ALL that happened last summer — in fact it's now exactly a year to the day when I first pulled up outside the caravan and Faye started drooling over Nathan.

This afternoon, she's stunning once more, in a long ivory satin dress, with her hair drawn into a chignon at the nape of her slender neck, perfectly revealing her flawless features. She looks every inch the successful fashion buyer she is.

Her life is still a frantic whirl — jetting off here, there and everywhere at the drop of a hat. Paris. New York. Rome.

Waiting in the church porch for our cue, her eyes are firmly fixed on the tall dark man, his back to us, waiting at the altar with his shorter, smoother-haired brother, who's also looking immaculate in honour of the occasion.

As tears fill my eyes there's the gloriously rich resonance of organ music. It sends shivers racing up my spine. Faye turns and her gaze locks into mine.

"You look simply beautiful, Erin," she whispers huskily, reaching out to adjust a fold of pale lace and smooth a strand of my sharply bobbed haircut, which reveals cheekbones I never knew I had until Josh did that first simple sketch.

"Ready, sweetheart?"

Nodding, I take my dad's arm as Faye ushers the rest of my escorts, especially the two mischievous tiny flower girls, into order. Then we begin the long walk down the flower-filled aisle to where Josh, Nathan's twin brother, is waiting for his bride.

Me! The once-plain-and-organised little nursing sister, who has blossomed like a flower since that first magical kiss.

It was on a star-filled night, sand between our bare toes, under a beaming moon.

"I fell in love with you at first sight," Josh had declared. "You were all pink and pretty and flustered. I was terrified that Nathan would make a move on you — or that you would make a beeline for him, like women usually do, especially when they found out he's a high-powered businessman!

"It's tough being the boring twin, who just paints pictures," Josh had finished, touchingly comically, and my heart had gone out to him. Completely.

* * * *

As for Faye and Nathan . . . well, there's definitely *something* between them. They date — on the rare occasions that they're both in the same town at the same time. And she never mentions any other boyfriends, the way she used to.

Josh says Nathan's changed, too — that he no longer wines and dines a bevy of beauties on a regular basis.

We're at the altar now and, over my wonderfully good-looking, soon-to-be-husband's head, I can see his best man's dark eyes settle on my chief bridesmaid.

And I know, I just *know*, Faye's wearing the same soppy expression.

We are twins, after all!

A soft sigh of sheer happiness escapes my lips. She's always wanted the best for me. And I want *exactly* the same for her.

There's nothing like a wedding to bring two people to their senses, to make them realise that work isn't everything. Witnessing other people's sheer joy in making a solemn vow to one another can have a knock-on effect.

So, as Faye has said on more than one occasion, "Who knows . . .?" ❏

E VIE cradled Maria in her arms and gently kissed her soft, silky forehead. It was like a dream come true — a baby of her own, after all these years of waiting. She lowered the sleeping baby into the cot and covered her with the soft blanket. Gently, she traced the tip of her finger across the little daughter's soft cheek. Then she straightened up and stood by the cot, watching her sleeping. Her daughter. Hers and Dan's.

The miracle of human life overwhelmed her, and she vowed that Maria, unlike her, would always know what it was like to have a mother's love.

**by
Kay
Harborne**

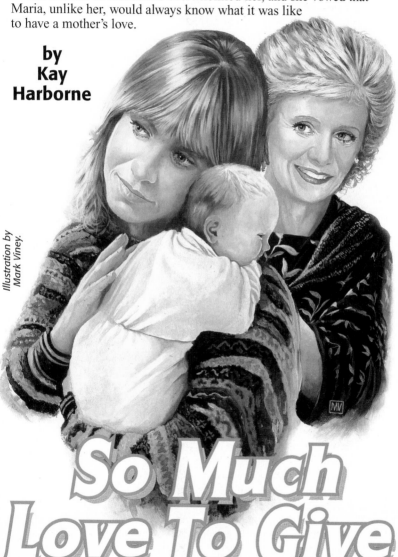

Illustration by
Mark Viney.

So Much Love To Give

Her own mother had been a young, single parent, unable to cope, and Evie had been brought up in a string of different homes. Her mother had come to visit her now and again, always promising to bring Evie home as soon as she got straight — but she died when Evie was only ten, so she'd never been able to keep that promise.

When she met Dan, it was the first time in her life Evie had encountered solid, unconditional love. They'd longed for a baby to make their family complete, and there were times when she thought it would never happen. But after four long, agonising years, Maria had arrived.

"Is she asleep?" Dan peered around the bedroom door, and Evie nodded, her finger to her lips.

Dan hastily disappeared again. She heard the soft thud of his footsteps as he walked across the hall and down the stairs.

SHE looked around the bedroom, taking in the Teddy bear wallpaper, matching curtains and lampshade, the pale lemon carpet, the fluffy white rug, the swinging cot with the frilly drapes . . .

Then there was the big pink Teddy bear sitting in the corner, and the toybox, overflowing with an assortment of baby toys . . .

They'd worked hard to transform the spare bedroom into this bright, friendly nursery. They hadn't wanted to know the baby's sex, hence the neutral colours.

With a final, lingering look at the sleeping baby, Evie tiptoed out of the room and went down into the lounge. She sank down on the sofa just as Dan came in from the kitchen with two mugs of hot chocolate.

"I thought you needed this. You look all in." He handed one of the mugs to her.

"I am a bit tired," Evie acknowledged. "I hadn't realised just how exhausting a young baby can be. Not that I'm grumbling," she added hastily.

"As if!" Dan smiled, placing his hand on hers. "You know I'll do anything to help, don't you? I don't mind. I can bottle feed, change nappies, the lot. I grew up in a large family, remember?"

"There's no need," Evie said stiffly. "I can manage, really I can."

Dan looked as if he was about to say something, then stopped.

"Drink up, then off to bed with you," he said softly. "Get your rest while you can."

"OK." Evie yawned, only too pleased to comply.

As soon as her head touched the pillow she fell into an exhausted, dreamless sleep, broken what seemed moments later by the sound of a baby crying.

Automatically, she pulled back the duvet to get out of bed.

"You go back to sleep. I'll go to her," Dan mumbled sleepily.

"No, you stay there," she said firmly. "I want to go."

She'd padded across the bedroom floor before Dan could protest further.

"There, there, darling. Mummy's here." She cradled the crying baby. "I'll always be here for you, no matter how tired I am. I'll never let you down. Never."

It took an hour to settle Maria, and she was awake again at half-past five. Evie was in the nursery, changing her, when she heard the alarm go off. Ten minutes later, Dan came in, half-dressed.

"I was wondering if my blue shirt was washed," he said. "I don't mind ironing it if . . ."

"Oh, Dan, I haven't even got round to doing our washing yet." Evie stifled a yawn. "Maria gets through so many things that the machine seems to be on all day just coping with her washing. I'm really sorry. I'll do it today, I promise."

"No problem, I can wear my white one."

Evie could tell he was disappointed.

"Oh — your presentation! I forgot —" She forced back the tears that had been flowing too readily to her eyes just lately.

She so wanted to be a good mother to Maria and a good wife to Dan, but it was hard to cope . . .

* * * *

"I'm worried about Evie," Dan told his mother. He'd popped in to see her on the way home from work. "She looks so tired and worn out. I've offered to help, honest I have, but she insists on doing everything herself."

"It's only natural for a new mother to feel like that." Janice handed him a mug of tea. "Evie's just trying to be a good mum — and probably trying harder than most, seeing as she never really had a mother of her own."

"I know, Mum. That's what I keep telling myself. But Maria's my baby, too. I *want* to help look after her."

"Give it time, love," his mother said. "It'll sort itself out, you'll see."

DAN was late, Evie thought, as she turned down the casserole bubbling in the oven. Still, it gave her time to tidy around, and Maria was still asleep, thank goodness.

Just then, she heard Dan's key.

"Sorry I'm late, love. I popped in to see Mum," he said.

"How is she?" Evie came out of the kitchen to greet him.

"Fine. She sends her love." He looked around. "Where's Maria?"

"Asleep in her cot. Have you had a good day?"

"Not bad — I think the presentation went well." He kissed her. "Something smells nice."

"I've made your favourite — liver and bacon casserole. You go and freshen up and I'll dish it out."

"Lovely! I'll go and have a quick shower then. I won't be long."

She'd just laid the table when Dan came down, carrying a gurgling Maria.

"Look who's just woken up." He grinned.

"Here, let me take her while you have your dinner. You must be starving." Evie quickly took the baby.

Was that a hurt look in Dan's eyes? But then it was gone.

"What about *your* dinner?" he asked.

"I'll eat it later — I'll see to Maria first."

Dan hesitated, then shrugged.

"OK. Well, I don't fancy eating at the table by myself so I'll take a tray and watch the news."

Evie felt a bit guilty. Their evening meal used to be their special time of day. But she didn't seem to have time to sit and eat a meal any more . . .

When Dan had left for work the next morning, Evie resolved to have a good tidy up, starting with the mound of dirty washing. Maria had woken for a feed earlier and gone straight back to sleep, so Evie managed to load the washing machine, tidy the bathroom, make the bed and wash up before the baby woke again.

She'd just finished dressing Maria when the doorbell rang.

"Oh, no!" Evie groaned. Still in her pyjamas and unshowered, she looked a mess. She decided to ignore it, but the letterbox opened and she heard her mother-in-law call.

"Evie! Are you there, love?"

Sighing, she strapped Maria into her seat and went to answer the door.

"Hello, love. I was just passing, so I thought I'd pop in to see how you are."

Janice gave her a warm, friendly smile.

"I was just about to take a shower. I wanted to get a few jobs done first," Evie gabbled, conscious of how dishevelled she looked.

"There's never enough hours in the day when you've a young baby, is

---

Barry Mill, Angus

RECENTLY restored to full working order, the three-storey mill, which overlooks the quiet village of Barry, near Carnoustie, dates from 1814 and is the last water-driven mill in Angus.

A mill has stood on this site since the 16th century and, at one time, there would have been hundreds serving the local communities. Indeed, the mill was at the very heart of village life.

Now a working museum, Barry Mill provides people today with a glimpse of how their ancestors lived and worked — opening a fascinating doorway on our past.

BARRY MILL, ANGUS: J CAMPBELL KERR

85

there, dear?" Janice put down her bag and took off her coat. "You pop up and have your shower, and I'll make us a nice coffee."

"Thank you. I won't be long. Maria's in her chair."

"Lovely. I can spoil her a bit!" Janice walked into the lounge.

"And how's my little darling today, then?"

Evie had a very quick shower. She towel-dried her hair and tied it back with a scrunchie, then hurried downstairs to find Janice rocking Maria in her arms as she sang to her.

Two mugs of coffee, and a plate of biscuits which Evie knew she hadn't bought, were on the coffee table.

"Thank you for looking after her," Evie said as she held out her arms for the baby. "And for the biscuits."

"Hmm." Janice looked at her. "You're tired, love. Why don't you go and lie down for an hour? I'll look after Maria."

"No!" She hadn't meant to say it so sharply, and her mother-in-law stared at her in surprise.

"I can manage, honestly!" Evie assured her, more calmly.

"I never said you couldn't, love. It's just that I know how demanding babies are." Janice reached over and touched Evie's hand.

"You don't have to manage all by yourself, you know. Maria's got a dad, and grandparents, too. She's got a whole family to look after her."

"But I'm her mother!" Evie's voice wobbled.

"I know, but you're not Superwoman. None of us are, love." Janice stood up and smoothed down her skirt.

"Anyway, I must go now. I've got some shopping to do." She looked tentatively at Evie. "I could take Maria with me, if you like. Give you the chance to get a few jobs done?"

Evie hesitated. That *would* give her time to catch up. And she knew Maria would be in safe hands.

"I'd really love to take her," Janice coaxed. "I haven't had a chance to show off my new granddaughter yet."

She really meant it, Evie realised.

"That would be great. Thank you," she said. "I'll just get her ready."

"Really? That's wonderful!" Janice's face broke into a huge smile. "I won't be long, love. And don't worry, Maria will be perfectly safe with me."

EVIE managed to peg the washing on the line, vacuum and clean the kitchen before Janice came back with a wide-awake Maria. "Has she been OK?" Evie took the baby out of the pram and cuddled her.

"She's been perfect!" Janice beamed. "As good as gold. And everyone said how beautiful she was."

"Would you like to stay for a coffee?"

"I'd love to, but let me make it while you feed Maria," Janice said.

"She looks like she's about to erupt!"

Maria was puckering her little face into a scowl. Suddenly, she let rip with a loud wail.

"It's a good job I've a bottle ready." Evie grinned.

By the time Janice left, Evie felt a lot better. They'd ended up having two cups of coffee while they chattered about Maria, and Dan and his brothers and sisters when they were babies.

Janice told her all sorts of things about the scrapes they'd got into and how Dan had screamed every night for the first six months . . .

"I'd never have managed without my mum," Janice confessed. "She'd take Dan off for a couple of hours every afternoon so I could get my head down. She helped me keep my sanity."

Evie was thoughtful when Janice finally left.

When Dan came home that night, Evie was humming to herself as she laid the table. The baby was lying in her seat, chuckling.

"How are my two favourite girls, then?" He leaned over to kiss Evie, then Maria.

"Fine. Your mother popped round and took Maria to the shops with her while I tidied up."

Dan looked at her, surprised. She'd never let Maria out of her sight before.

"Mum would enjoy that," he said. "She's been dying for a chance to show off Maria! She loves being a granny, you know."

"We had a good natter, too." Evie grinned. "Evidently you were a right little terror when you were a boy!"

"Never! I was the perfect child!" He grinned back. Then Maria started grumbling, and Dan picked her up.

"What's all this in aid of, then?" he said softly.

"It's her bedtime," Evie told him. "Suppose I see to her while you have a shower? Then we can have dinner together."

*　　*　　*　　*

It had been nice to have dinner together again, Evie thought, as she lay in bed that night. And she'd enjoyed Janice's visit, too. Maybe she should let her mother-in-law help a bit more . . .

Then her eyes closed despite themselves.

When she woke, it was already light. Dan's side of the bed was empty. What time was it? She looked at the clock in panic.

Seven o'clock! She'd slept all through the night! Maria must have woken and she hadn't even heard her . . .

She pulled on her dressing-gown and hurried across the landing. The bedroom door was open, and she could hear Dan singing a lullaby. She peered in.

Dan was standing by the window, rocking Maria in his arms and singing softly. As he half-turned to look down at the baby, the proud, tender look on his face brought a lump to her throat.

"We waited a long time for you, darling, Mummy and I," he said softly. "Don't worry, we're going to look after you. We'll make sure you're always happy, because we both love you very much."

We both love you. The words echoed in Evie's mind. In her joy at having a baby, and her anxiety never to fail Maria, as her own mother had failed her, Evie had forgotten one vital thing.

Maria wasn't just *her* baby. She was Dan's, too. She had a mother and a father. And she needed both their love. What was it Janice had said? *Maria has a whole family of people who love her . . .*

As she watched Dan put the baby gently back in the cot, Evie realised what she'd done. She'd been shutting Dan out of her life — hers and Maria's.

"D AN," she said softly, and he looked up, startled. "I didn't want to wake you when you've been looking so tired," he said defensively, and her heart went out to him.

"I was, but I feel better now." Evie smiled, walking over to join him. "Did she wake very early?"

"About six."

They gazed down at the sleeping baby.

"I didn't mean to shut you out," Evie said softly. "I just didn't want anyone to think I couldn't look after her . . . that I couldn't cope."

"Like your mother, you mean?" Dan put his arm around her shoulder.

Evie nodded numbly.

"You know —" Dan held her close "— your mum probably didn't have anyone to help her look after you. She was really young, wasn't she?" He put his fingers under her chin and gently lifted it up. "I'm sure she loved you very, very much, and wanted to look after you."

"I guess you're right," Evie said softly.

"And, Evie . . ."

She saw the love in his eyes.

"You don't have to be a perfect wife and mother. I don't care if my shirts aren't ironed! I'm just happy to have you and Maria. We're a family at last."

A family. It was all she had ever wanted.

"I know," she said softly, looking up at him.

"Now, suppose we let my parents look after Maria for a couple of hours this evening while we go out for a meal?"

For a moment, Evie hesitated. Then she smiled at him.

"They'll love having her, won't they? And it would be nice to relax and spend a few hours on our own . . . It's time I let the rest of Maria's family love her, too."

"Thank you, darling." He kissed her, and she touched his cheek.

"I love you, Dan. And so does our daughter." ❏

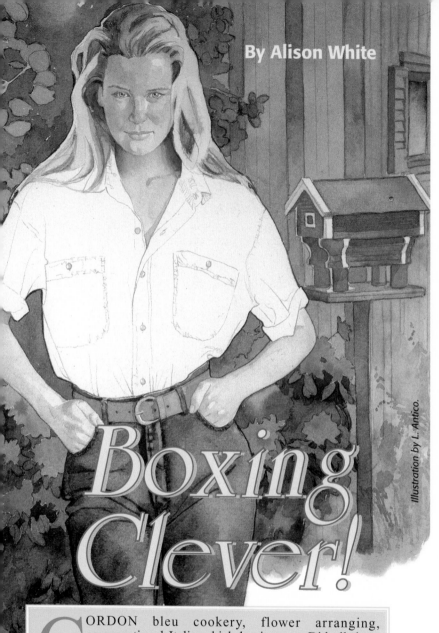

By Alison White

Illustration by L. Antico.

Boxing Clever!

CORDON bleu cookery, flower arranging, conversational Italian, kick boxing . . . Did all these classes ever get filled? I was stunned to learn from the local paper how much went on at the college down the road in the evenings.

"You've been on your own too long," my sister, Linda, said darkly. "You should do a class or something. It's all work and no play for you, Heather. You need to get out and meet people."

"You mean men," I said, scowling.

But she insisted she didn't.

"Just new people. Open yourself up a bit. Although if you do think you're ready to start dating again . . ."

I would have been happy to date again if I met someone nice. But I didn't dare admit that to Linda, or she'd parade men in front of me night and day.

"Well, you could try car maintenance," she suggested, narrowing her eyes at me.

I knew it was a test. I didn't flinch.

She lifted the paper again, disappointed I hadn't taken the bait.

"It'll be full of women with the same idea anyway."

"In that case," I said, "maybe I should do flower arranging in case the principle is reversed."

It was always the same if Linda was involved. What started off as an idle thought would always turn into a full-scale military operation.

"I see lots of men all day anyway," I reminded her. "I work in a florist's. They're always coming into the shop. Late on Fridays, usually."

She gave me that pitying look again.

"Yes, but they're buying flowers for the women in their lives, aren't they? You'll never meet anyone there, Heather."

I opened my mouth to tell her I wasn't trying to meet anyone, but Linda spoke first.

"I think kick boxing," she said, grinning at me over the paper. "It reduces aggression, gets the adrenaline going and is marvellous for your hamstrings. It tones them."

"My hams are pretty well strung as they are," I argued, looking down at my legs — I presumed that was where hamstrings were.

"And I'll come with you," she finished.

I sighed with relief. Linda doesn't like being out of breath for more than thirty seconds. She was sure to give up easily, and then she'd be off my case.

I TOOK one look at my fellow kick boxers and wanted to run for cover. I was too intimidated to say hello, let alone engage in some sort of combat sport.

"So how long have you been interested in this kind of thing?" the tutor asked.

"Since Linda made me — ow!" I said, rubbing my ribs where my sister had jabbed me.

"We thought it would be a good way of keeping fit," Linda broke in smoothly. "And learning technical skills at the same time."

That was the kind of answer Rick approved of. And Linda approved of him, I could tell.

Boxing Clever!

As a class we stretched and warmed up. I don't think people normally fall over when they're warming up, but Linda was trying to impress and wasn't concentrating. The next minute, she was on the floor.

I rushed over to help. Some mean part of me hoped she might have to be checked out at Casualty so I'd have to go with her and escape. But she got up again.

"We'll practise falling properly, then break for five minutes," Rick said.

I edged to the back of the room. I didn't want to fall — not even properly. Linda was still purring at Rick and oblivious to me, so I slipped out of the door.

"Lost?" a voice said, as I collided with its owner.

"Sorry." We both spoke at once.

"It's not for me," I said, pointing at the kick boxing room.

"Not for me, either," the man agreed, pointing at the room he'd just left. "Trouble is, I'm the teacher."

I laughed.

"Only joking. We could nip off for a coffee if you like," he said. "Or are you going to bite the bullet and go back in?"

"The only thing I'll bite is a biscuit," I said. "Coffee sounds wonderful."

We were first in the queue, and soon I was telling Tim how this had all been Linda's idea.

"You shouldn't waste your money, though," he said. "Why not transfer?"

"Would they let me at this stage?"

"I will." He grinned, then admitted he was the administrator.

"I thought you were the same as me. Backing out of a class with horror!"

"I was." He shuddered. "I'd just taken some paperwork to the tutor and got a shock. Art class."

"Oh?" I brightened. "I always liked art at school."

"This is advanced," Tim said. "You might say Adult Art. They were doing 'life' drawing. I didn't know where to look."

"You mean no . . . er . . . clothes?"

"I do."

We were still laughing when Linda appeared.

"What happened to you? I thought it was great."

"It's not for me. Tim's going to sort me out with a transfer."

"To what?"

"Cordon bleu, maybe?" Tim suggested. "I've done the course myself. I could give you some tips."

"No kick boxing for you, then," Linda said, then melted away towards Rick.

"But maybe," Tim said slowly, "a kick start to something else . . . ?"

I raised my coffee cup. I'd certainly drink to that. ❏

PETER paused before slipping the postcards into the post-box to re-read the words his family had written to people back home.

Dear Dawn,
We're in Disneyland! Dad promised us that if it was the last thing he ever did, we were going to go to America and Florida and Orlando and Disney. It's very hot. The grass is funny. There are hundreds of good things in the shops.
Love, Rachel.

Hi, Robert!
The Frog wants to go to the Magic Kingdom tomorrow and do all the girlie rides. Dad says we have to wait until Friday to go to EPCOT.
The hotel is brilliant! There's a monorail that goes right through the building!
It took nine hours to get here. Dad had a headache when we landed. Mam said it was because of the flight.
Gotta go. Bet you wish you were here!
Love, Ben.

Dear Millie,
I hope you and Dad are well. The flight was far better than I expected. There was so much for me to do that I forgot to be frightened!
Peter was very tired. Rachel led him round everywhere by the hand. They bought me perfume. I told Peter off for spending but he just laughed and said, "What's money?" The kids played Scrabble most of the flight. Peter fell asleep in my lap.
Your loving daughter, Margaret.

The card his daughter, Rachel, had chosen had a picture of Winnie-the-Pooh and Tigger in front of a blue-grey castle. The holiday was costing a fortune, but he knew he had never spent money more wisely.

Before they'd left, he'd told his wife, Margaret, that this would be a once-in-a-lifetime trip and not to

worry about the expense.

"It's all taken care of," he'd said.

The look on the kids' faces when he told them was sheer joy.

He watched three-year-old Toby pressing his face against a toy-shop window in the hotel concourse. There was a time when he might have been impatient, but not now, not any more. He was on holiday, and he wanted to wear a silly hat and look gormless!

Tonight, he would make up another story for the kids and sit on that huge hotel bed with their spiky arms and legs hooked into him. He would whisper little messages to Margaret as they fell asleep in each other's arms, while the kids slept soundly on the other bed.

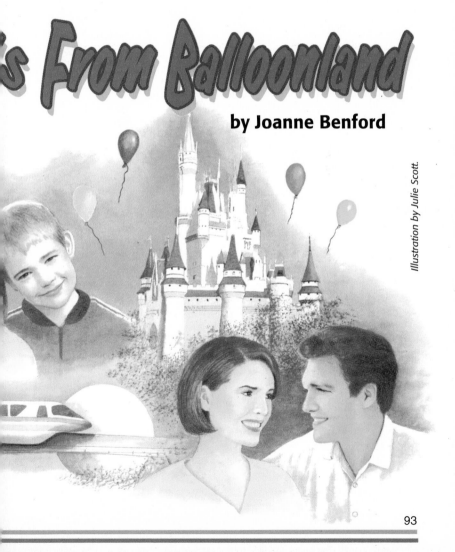

's From Balloonland

by Joanne Benford

Illustration by Julie Scott.

"Dad?" a little voice asked.

Peter looked down at Rachel.

"Can we have balloons? Like those?"

They were large, bright, helium-filled silver balls, stretching towards the sky on soft string. They bought three. Margaret tied them — one each — to small wrists. Immediately, Toby began to pick at his.

"Don't!" Margaret said. "You'll lose it!"

"Free it, don't you mean?" Peter said softly.

Margaret glanced at him. He looked dreamy and lost.

They found a café and sat outside, enjoying their drinks in the sunshine.

"It's pretty!" Rachel said, when a small bird appeared on their table, pecking at crumbs.

Toby was the first to lose his balloon. When he burst into tears, Margaret sat down and held him. Behind her, Rachel let her balloon go, too, watched it float into the sky, then began to cry like her brother.

Peter pulled his little girl to him. He felt giddy, but he swept her up and wrapped her in his arms, spinning around, her gold head pressed into his neck.

"Hey, sweetheart," he said, the world still turning. "There's a good brave girl. Fancy you knowing about Balloonland."

Rachel sniffed.

"I did tell you, didn't I?" Peter asked, wiping away her tears. "About Balloonland."

She shook her head.

He called all the children over, and they sat together on the grass.

"I told you, Ben, didn't I?" Peter asked his eldest son. "Last year, I think."

But Ben shook his head.

"Well, I never!" Peter said. Then, turning to Margaret, he said, "They don't know about Balloonland. Well, I never!"

He leaned back, his hands clasped behind his head, sun in his face. The kids were leaning forward.

"Well, I never!" he repeated and closed his eyes.

"Tell, tell!" Toby squeaked.

"Tell us, Daddy," Rachel said, joining in.

"Oh, Dad!" Ben said.

Peter opened one eye.

"I think you'd better." Margaret smiled.

"When balloons are born," Peter began to explain as he sat up, "they are flat and sad and don't know what to do. If people don't blow them up, they never get to feel big or bouncy or pretty."

He paused and, seeing their spellbound expressions, continued.

"You know when you see balloons in their packets?"

Toby was nodding, his eyes wide.

"They're flat and they don't smell nice and they're all dusty." Peter smiled.

"Well, they're waiting to be blown up so they can do things, like go flying in the sky.

"We all know balloons are very special things," Peter continued. "That's why we have them at birthday parties and at Christmas. And people want to keep their balloons. They think that, if they keep their balloon, everyone will carry on having a lovely time. But . . ."

The children looked at him expectantly.

"Balloons were made to fly," Peter explained. "They want to go back to Balloonland."

"Balloonland?" Ben repeated.

"Well, you know how balloons float up and stick to the ceiling?" Peter paused.

The children were all nodding.

"Well, they're trying to go home, to Balloonland." He pulled them to him, the warmth of his family engulfing him. "You see, balloons are like very special birds. They can't sing like birds but they make people sing sometimes. They come alive for birthdays, but then, afterwards, they want to go."

"But why don't they want to stay here, Dad?" Rachel asked, entirely caught up in the story.

"If you keep a balloon, what happens? It goes all droopy and wrinkly because it's sad. If you keep a balloon for a very long time, all its balloon-ness leaks out and it goes to sleep again."

Toby looked faintly worried.

"But if you let a balloon go," Peter added quickly, "it goes up in the sky, straight off to Balloonland. And if a balloon gets to Balloonland it never comes down, because it's happy and bouncy and can fly for ever.

"Balloonland is full of every single balloon that you could ever imagine. Red ones, yellow ones, blue ones, fat ones, wiggly ones . . .

"So, just think," Peter finished softly. "Right now, in Balloonland there's —"

"My balloon!" Toby said.

"And mine!" Rachel added.

IT was later when Ben released his balloon. Peter and Margaret exchanged amused glances, realising they could hardly chastise him now, especially since Ben looked extremely pleased with himself.

After lunch, Margaret bought three more balloons and diligently fixed them to three wrists. Just as diligently, the cords were loosened and the balloons released.

Peter groaned, his eyes rolling, but the kids were already clamouring for more, and Margaret thought it funny.

"Six dollars!" She giggled. "How are you going to get out of this one, maestro?"

Peter was a little tired, so he found a seat, then called the children to

Loch Ness

SCOTLAND's scenery is truly beautiful — that goes without saying — but there are always those that feel they can improve on perfection! This was certainly the case when American film-makers came to Loch Ness to shoot the 1994 film of the same name.

The famous Loch wasn't quite what the film-makers had in mind. They wanted a lochside village, too, and so added footage from Loch Torridon to that of Loch Ness.

The film — which starred Ted Danson and Joely Richardson — told the story of a disillusioned American scientist (Danson) who is sent to Scotland in search of . . . You guessed it! The Loch Ness monster.

During his stay, Danson encounters all sorts of eccentric Scottish characters, including one played by Ian Holm and, most importantly, Nessie hersel

Joely Richardson's character i the film is the proprietor of a small hotel at Loch Ness. These scenes were actually shot in the tiny village of Lower Diabaig, which is about fifty miles north of the Loch. It's easy to see why the film-makers chose this particular area. It's a real gem, with some of the Scotland's mo spectacular scenery.

It's not surprising that a film has been made of the Scottish legend of the Loch Ness monster. Ever since the first recorded sighting of the Beasti in a biography of St Columba, written in the 7th century, tourists and locals alike have been fascinated by this endurin enigma.

him again. He needed to explain about balloon jams.

"When balloons get to Balloonland, sometimes there are lots arriving at the same time, so they have to wait," he began. "The danger is, they could float down again while they are waiting. That's why we keep them on strings for a while, so we can let them go every now and then. To stop the jams."

Peter looked to his wife for reassurance.

Margaret smiled as she told the children that, tomorrow, they could keep their balloons all day. Then they could set them free in the evening, after the balloon rush-hour. She was still smiling, the sun shining through her hair.

Peter continued, telling the children that jams happened because Balloonland only had one way in. The Balloonland bosses wanted to make another way in, but balloons didn't know how to build entrances.

"So, really, they could do with some grown-up humans to do the building for them," he explained. "But it's very hard for humans to get back from Balloonland, so they have trouble getting volunteers."

As they walked back towards the exits at the end of the day, a balloon sailed past and over them. Somewhere in the distance, a child was crying,

Loch Ness.

Ted Danson.

On The Silver Screen

but Rachel, Ben and Toby cheered.

Margaret turned to Peter and smiled.

"You clever thing," she said. "I love you."

Peter was soundly asleep when they arrived back at the resort. Margaret woke him and he walked sleepily to the hotel for dinner. The next morning, she had trouble waking him, but he eventually stirred and followed her down to breakfast.

The children were asking about balloons so he said he would ring up and get a traffic report. He left them, used the phone and then came back, nodding to Margaret and telling the children that Balloonway One was absolutely chock-a-block with balloons.

"Apparently," he said, "there were a lot of parties in Australia last night and they are still dealing with a back-log from Christmas. They said they could probably manage a few balloons late this afternoon."

They stayed another week, slept late every morning, and swam lazily in the hotel pool as the evenings drew in. Then, their fortnight was over, and Nana and Grandpa Bill were coming to Orlando to take the children back to Grandpa's farm.

When they met, the two women embraced. Bill shook Peter's hand before pulling him close and hugging him silently.

The grandparents and children flew back home the following night. Peter tried hard to keep the mood light as they prepared to board their plane. Earlier, they had let five balloons off to a count of "one, two, three," and cheered as they sailed into space.

Margaret had chosen to dress the three of them in Mickey Mouse clothing and little Toby even wore a black big-eared cap.

When it was actually time to go, they hugged, first as a family, then Peter held each child in turn, smelling them, feeling the breath on his face, sensing their heartbeats. After holding Ben, he stood back and held his hand out seriously, like a man.

Margaret drove the car south to Miami while Peter slept. They had booked into a wonderful hotel at the head of the Keys and, the following day, they walked hand in hand on quiet, printless sand. They were caught in a sudden rainstorm but chose to enjoy it, laughing, their heads back savouring its warmth.

THAT afternoon, they drove towards Key West, stopping at a little harbour where Margaret ate from an incredible seafood buffet. Peter had no appetite, but they sipped wine together and talked quietly.

That night, they were asleep at six, Peter cradled against her chest, her gentle hands stroking his head. The next day, they did nothing but lie together on top of the sheets, a copper fan thudding above them.

At their destination, they ate in romantic restaurants. In the evenings, they drifted along to the pier to watch the sunset. They stopped to buy books. Peter chose three, stopped, then replaced two. And every night Margaret held him — they were closer than they'd ever been.

On their last day in the Keys, Peter found a painting, depicting balloons over Paris. Then, from a surprised shopkeeper, he bought a complete supply of postcards, all of balloons.

While Margaret drove north, Peter wrote carefully on card after card. Each message was different, each card dated oddly.

By the time they arrived back on the mainland, he was tired and his writing was less fluid. They stopped in Miami. Peter was asleep again so Margaret arranged the check-in.

They flew to the clinic next day. While their plane drifted in to land, he explained again how she should use the cards. The children would receive one every birthday, one at Christmas, one on the day their father was born. He told her that Ben, Rachel and Toby should stay children as long as possible.

He was going away, but they would know how to contact him.

After all, someone had to help build the new entrance at the other end of Balloonway One. If he volunteered, the children could still send him messages any time they wanted. All they had to do was attach a note to a balloon, addressing it *care of Balloonland,* then set it free . . . ❏

By
Sheri Davies

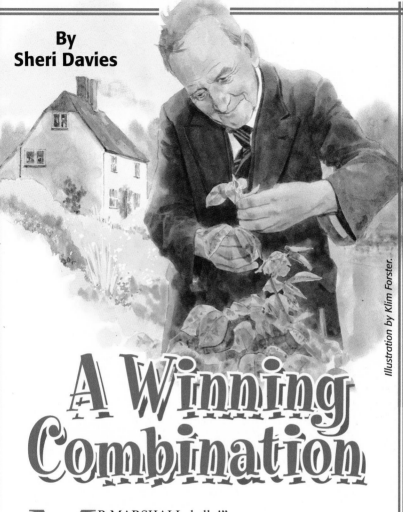

Illustration by Klim Forster.

A Winning Combination

"MR MARSHALL, hello!"

Kenneth Marshall was kneeling on the garden path, jabbing dispiritedly at the soil with a trowel. Beside him was a box of bulbs. He straightened up and peered through the gap in the fence. Oliver Morgan was grinning back at him.

"Is it that time again? I must say, you're doing a grand job!" The younger man raised his mug of steaming coffee in salute.

"Don't get me started . . ." the older man growled.

"Pardon?" Oliver put down his coffee and edged closer to the fence.

"I'm going to let you into a secret," Kenneth muttered, looking around. "I've never liked gardening."

"But . . . I've always thought . . . you spend so much time . . ."

Kenneth looked around again. Oliver crept closer to the fence.

"I only ever did it to please the father-in-law. He didn't think a lot of me when I was courting his lass, so I pretended to be as keen on gardening as he was. I've had to do the blasted borders ever since!"

"You're not going to tell me that your father-in-law's still going strong somewhere?" Oliver replied in amazement. Kenneth was in his late sixties.

"*He's* not," Kenneth said grimly, "but my daughter is. If I stop doing the garden she'll think it's because I'm not able. She'll have me selling up and moving in with her faster than you can say . . . narcissus."

Oliver had met Sylvie.

"Ah!" he said knowingly. "I'll leave you to it, then."

Kenneth had had enough by the early afternoon, so he got out the car and drove into town. It was a blustery March afternoon, with just a spattering of rain in the air. He pulled his coat closer around his neck.

He had nothing in particular to buy and nowhere in particular to go but he liked to get out of the house sometimes. He gazed into the warm, brightly-lit stores and blanched at the prices.

Suddenly, something fawn and very leggy shot past him. He spun round to see a large greyhound bounding around the corner towards the main road.

He walked briskly after it. He could see where the dog had gone by the way the heads of the shoppers jerked around as it loped past them. A crowd was gathering around one particular store.

Kenneth looked up at the sign. *M. Abel* — it was Michael Abel's; gents outfitters. The shop front had a narrow window with two glass doors on either side, which stayed open whatever the weather. Two lads were standing at one of the doors and Kenneth peered in through the other one.

There, at the back of the shop, was the greyhound, its flanks heaving. Suddenly, it launched itself towards the doors.

"Here, Grandad," one of the boys called, "you watch that door and we'll watch this one."

"Grandad!" Kenneth muttered in disgust, crouching down nevertheless, ready to catch the dog should it come his way. Knowing his luck, it would — and it did! Deftly, he put out his left knee to block its exit. With one hand, he grasped the creature's collar, and with the other he pulled off his tie, to use for a lead.

"All right, Grandad?" The boys were grinning at him.

Kenneth fastened the tie around the collar and went to hand the dog back to them, but they skipped off.

"Hoi!" he bellowed. "What about the . . .?"

But he only caught the distant hoot of their laughter as they disappeared into the crowd.

He looked down at the dog.

"Well, I'll be blowed! I thought I was helping them and they thought they were helping me."

The dog looked up at him, its tongue lolling out comically.

He took the animal back down the side street where he had first seen it and knocked on a few doors.

"Anyone recognise this greyhound?" he asked.

But nobody did. He trailed around Castle Street and up Delaney Road, but got the same answer.

The wind was whipping up now and the rain was starting to sting his hands. He looked at the dog, noticing the rain running down its sides.

"We can't go on like this or we'll both get pneumonia. Let's get you to the car," he decided.

They shivered in the car for a few minutes while Kenneth wondered what to do next.

"A nice cup of tea will help me think," he confided in the animal, setting off for home.

The dog was soon dozing on a spare blanket in front of the fire. Kenneth gazed down at it, a steaming mug of tea in his hands.

"You've a nice enough nature," he said, reaching down to stroke the dog's silky ears. It blinked up at him gratefully and Kenneth chuckled.

"No good making eyes at me, miss. First thing in the morning, we're off to the police station to find your rightful owner. But what am I going to call you in the meantime?"

The dog yawned. It had had a busy day, and now it was warm and sleepy.

Kenneth stroked its silky head and mused to himself.

"Michael Abel's place. It's got to be Mabel, hasn't it?"

I HAVEN'T heard from Dad for days," Kenneth's daughter, Sylvie, fretted.

Her husband turned to the sports page.

"I shouldn't worry about him," he commented, without looking up, "it's not as though he's frail or anything."

"He's a pensioner!"

"Just. And a very active one at that."

Sylvie whisked a casserole from the freezer and a packet of doughnuts from the kitchen cupboard.

"I'm going round there," she declared.

"Just give him a ring, love. Don't haunt the poor man," Tony added under his breath.

"I heard that!" she muttered as she dialled her father's number. "Danny, do your homework," she barked at her son. "Tony, make him do

View of Morven Hills from shore of Loch Linnhe.

his homework. Dad! How are you? Yes, I know. You what? Tony!" she yelled holding the receiver to her chest, "Dad's caught a greyhound!"

"I didn't know he could run that fast!" Tony and Danny smothered their giggles, and Sylvie rolled her eyes heavenwards.

"Don't go away, Dad, I'm coming right over."

She banged the phone down. Fifteen minutes later, Kenneth opened the door to his voluble daughter and excited grandson.

"Where is it?" Danny barged past him into the front room. "And how did you catch it?"

"She's in there and she's called Mabel. It was just like being back in goal again and waiting for a penalty, Danny. There I was, standing in the doorway trying to decide which way she was going to go, and she

102

High Summer

THE bare hills rise beyond the scented pines,
  No secrets, now, they hold.
Their barren faces, scarred by furrowed lines,
Have suddenly grown old.

The sluggish burns meander through the peat,
The forest trails are dry.
And lochans shimmer, hazy in the heat,
Beneath a changeless sky.

Yet starry flowers, too numerous to name,
Still light the moorland ways.
And hardy rhododendron's rosy flame
Burns on the arid braes.

And though the sun-baked mountain summits stand
Stripped to the bone and bare,
Yet Mothers Nature's ever-lavish hand
Spreads colour everywhere!

                       — Brenda G. Macrow.

Dennis Hardley.

was hurtling towards me. Luckily, we both went the same way and I blocked her with my knee."

"She's a beaut!" the boy exclaimed, flinging his arms around Mabel's strong yet slender neck.

"Danny, mind!" his mother cautioned. "She might bite."

"Rubbish," her father retorted. "She hasn't got a bad bone in her."

Mabel tapped at his hand with her wet nose and he stroked her absent-mindedly.

"Made herself at home, I see." Sylvie took in the two glowing bars of the electric fire, the blanket and packet of biscuits on the hearth. "I've brought you a casserole and some doughnuts. I'll leave them in the kitchen," she said, as she disappeared to make a pot of tea.

"What does Mabel eat?" Danny asked, gazing into the dog's golden-brown eyes.

"She's partial to steak and kidney pie."

"Oh, Dad! She'll be costing you a fortune!" Sylvie reappeared, and stood, hands on hips. "When are you going to get rid of her?"

A nervous smile twitched at the corner of Kenneth's mouth.

"Get rid of her?" he asked incredulously.

"You're certainly not going to keep her. Not a greyhound! If she doesn't eat you out of house and home she'll dig up the garden and, anyway, she'll need exercise — lots of it!" Sylvie finished.

Kenneth sighed. He'd enjoyed his afternoon with Mabel in front of the fire. The rain had been thrashing the window but they'd turned the fire up and put the radio on and it had been deliciously snug.

He knew, though, that she would have to go. It was a well-known fact that greyhounds required lots of exercise. He just wouldn't be up to it.

"I'll take her to the police station, tomorrow," he promised, looking his daughter firmly in the eye.

"Mum," Danny said as he struggled into his anorak after tea, "if Grandad doesn't want her . . ."

"Don't even think about it!" Sylvie fastened his zipper, swung her coat round her shoulders and marched towards the door. Danny let his mother go on ahead, then turned back to Kenneth.

"Grandad," he whispered.

Kenneth leant down to him.

"You know Mabel likes steak and kidney pie?"

The older man nodded.

"Well, she likes doughnuts, too!"

Kenneth winked at his grandson and saw them to the door.

THAT evening, Kenneth allowed the dog to sleep at the foot of his bed on her blanket.

"A bit of security for me," he told her as she gazed at him through half-closed eyes. "'Night, Mabel."

It was with a heavy heart that he took her to the police station next day. No-one had reported losing a greyhound so the duty sergeant told him that if Mabel wasn't claimed she'd be sent to the rescue centre in the next town.

"'Bye, Mabel," Kenneth said sadly, as she turned to look at him over her shoulder. "You'll make someone a lovely pet."

The house seemed very empty when he got back. He folded up the blanket and picked up Mabel's water dish. He moved the sofa back to its original place and gave the place a good vacuuming. That would please Sylvie.

Then he sat down to a long afternoon in front of the television. But suddenly, snooker had lost its appeal.

Two days later, he decided that he would visit the rescue centre just to make sure Mabel was being properly looked after.

"I've come to see Mabel," he told the girl at the reception. "She's a greyhound. I found her. I expect someone's claimed her by now?"

The girl scanned her records.

"No, not yet. We find that greyhounds often get left. Would you like to see her?"

"Oh, yes!" Kenneth eagerly followed the girl into the kennel area. "But she's got such a lovely nature!"

The girl nodded.

"It's a shame. Greyhounds make good pets, really. Mabel would, too. She's into middle age so she's not too lively, but most people think of them as needing lots of walks. It's a myth, though, once the dog's retired."

Kenneth's eyes widened.

"Really?"

"That's right. And they don't need much grooming, either."

His face brightened further.

"And if no-one claims her?"

"Then she's up for re-homing!"

Suddenly, Kenneth hoped with all his heart that no-one would come for her.

* * * *

The week flew by and the weather brightened. Sylvie decided that it was time to look in on her father again, and took Danny along. They crunched their way along the gravel path to the back garden.

"Hello, Mr Morgan!" Sylvie said in surprise, as she spotted her father's neighbour. "Doing a bit of DIY?" She nodded at the hammer in his hand.

"Hello, Sylvie. Hi, Danny! We're just making sure the fences are secure."

"Fences?" She turned to face her father.

He shuffled his feet, glad that his next-door neighbour was there for moral support.

"That's right. It's Mabel," he explained. "She's back!"

Danny gave a whoop of joy.

"Why don't you go and let her out, son? She's in the kitchen," Kenneth said.

"Actually," Oliver mused, spying the bulbs and trowel on the path. "I don't really think you'll be needing those now, will you?"

Kenneth looked at them and then caught on.

"Oh, no! You're right there. Well, Sylvie," he said, glancing at his daughter's aghast expression. "You were the one who said that Mabel will be digging up the borders!"

"But, Dad. Your gardening! It's your passion . . ."

"Sacrifices," he said, shaking his head sadly, and privately vowing to treat his neighbour to the best bottle of whisky he could find. "We all have to make sacrifices." ❏

Follow Your Dream

I'LL never forget the day Toby introduced me to Sam, for it was the day I received my redundancy notice. The two events are linked for ever in my mind.

I was working at the till when they came to pay for their food. Toby introduced us in his usual, breezy, friendly way.

"Anna, meet Sam, an old mate of mine from the Navy. He's just sailed from Madeira."

But other than the fact that he had a nice smile, nothing else about Sam particularly registered with me. My mind was still reeling from the contents of that letter.

I could feel the envelope in my apron pocket, a continual reminder that its contents were about to tear my well-ordered, if boring, life apart.

Toby and Sam moved away to sit at a nearby table to eat their meal.

I'd worked at the café on the quay for ten years, working my way up to assistant manageress. It was a grand-sounding title for a mishmash of jobs — cooking, waitressing, washing-up, reception and working the till.

By Jennifer Bohnet

I quite enjoyed the variety of the work but, deep in my heart, I knew I could do more. But I've always lacked the necessary motivation. Dad had for ever been on at me to go to college and get some decent qualifications — start my own business, maybe.

But I've never been much of a risk-taker.

I remember thinking that perhaps losing my job would be good for me. It would force me to do something about my life, get out of the rut.

Of course, I'd known for months that the café was up for sale. But, like everyone else, I'd assumed the new owners would keep on the existing staff.

The letter informed me differently.

The café will be closed for modernisation for at least three months. All staff entitled to redundancy pay will receive it. When the business reopens as The Quayside CyberCafé, we shall engage new staff.

CyberCafé! Half the locals round here will thinks it's a CyderCafé spelled wrongly. They haven't a clue what a cybercafé is.

Now I was beginning to see that both Mum and Dad had been right. I should have moved on by now.

The thought of the redundancy money crossed my mind. How much would it be? A couple of thousand? Or just a few hundred? Knowing my luck that would be nearer the mark. It certainly wouldn't go far if I didn't get another job quickly.

The day of the letter dragged on. Inevitably, news had leaked out that the café was to close at the end of the week and a lot of the regulars were really upset.

"There's nowhere else on the quay to get a decent cuppa," they moaned.

Toby, returning to the counter for another cup of coffee, had tried to reassure me.

"You'll get another job, Anna. People are crying out for good staff like you."

I smiled at him gratefully. But, at forty-two, I wasn't nearly so sure.

THAT evening after work I walked home slowly along the quay towards the cottage my parents had left me. I could always sell the cottage and have a large lump sum to put with my redundancy money . . .

The cottage two doors down had been sold recently at a price that had seemed silly to us locals. It was currently being turned into yet another holiday home.

If I sold my cottage, surely there would be enough then to start a new life somewhere else. But did I have the courage? And where would I go?

I was deep in thought, oblivious to my surroundings, when I realised someone was calling my name.

"Anna! Anna!"

I turned and saw Sam, standing in the cockpit of a large sailing boat. He was holding a bottle of red wine.

"Hi, there. Care to come aboard for a drink?" he invited.

I hesitated a mere fraction of a second before taking Sam's outstretched hand and jumping on board.

"We'll have a glass of wine and then I'll give you the Grand Tour. It'll take all of five minutes!" he told me.

Three hours later, I was still on board. Sam was right. The tour of the yacht *had* only taken five minutes. The rest of the time we had simply talked and talked.

It was the first time in years I'd met a man who was interested in me. A man who was prepared to listen and offer the odd word of advice.

I learned a lot about Sam that evening, too.

A picture pinned up in the tiny gallery brought a proud admission from him.

"That's my daughter, Lola. Isn't she beautiful? Unfortunately her mother omitted to tell me about her until last year, so she grew up without me knowing her."

He'd been silent for a moment, studying the attractive teenage girl in the picture.

"But now we know about each other, we're making up for lost time. I'm setting off to see her again soon."

A feeling of disappointment ran through me. So he didn't plan to stay around. That was a shame. I'd had this fleeting feeling that we'd have got on really well.

But it was nice that he was making the effort to get to know his daughter . . . that he cared about her.

108

But then, as I found out over the next few days, Sam was a very caring man.

Not only did he walk me home that first evening, he turned up unexpectedly at the cottage the next day with a large bunch of flowers.

"Yellow flowers always look so vibrant and happy somehow. Just like you." He smiled.

I thought that was maybe stretching it a bit. That week in particular, I certainly was feeling anything but vibrant and happy. I was about to become unemployed, and I still hadn't decided what I was going to do with "the rest of my life", as the saying goes.

The flowers certainly made me feel better, though, as did Sam's invitation to go for a sail and have dinner on board that evening.

I couldn't remember the last time I'd gone sailing. But once on board the *Lovely Lady,* the memories came flooding back.

Casting off from the mooring, tightening the sail sheets as we cleared the harbour and pulling the sails up had once been a familiar routine to me. I was surprised at how many of the old skills I remembered.

"Take the helm, will you? I've got to go below for something." Sam disappeared into the bow of the yacht.

Sitting there, skimming across the water in the cool evening breeze, the floodgates of my memory opened.

I recalled the days Dad and I had spent on his small cabin cruiser, just cruising up and down the coast. The *One and Only* had been his pride and joy in his retirement.

When Sam returned, the tears were pouring down my cheeks. A reassuring arm went instantly around my shoulders.

"Anna, what is it?"

"Nothing." I shook my head. "It's just that I haven't been sailing since my dad died. I was just remembering some of our trips together." I smiled at him. "I'd also forgotten just how much I used to enjoy it."

"Why did you stop?"

"We couldn't afford to keep the boat after Dad died. Then Mum became ill shortly afterwards.

"There wasn't much time for sailing," I finished quietly.

With a comforting squeeze of my shoulder, Sam silently took the helm again.

We moored in a tiny deserted cove and companionably prepared dinner together. We ate out on deck as the water gently slapped against the hull and the breeze ruffled the halyards against the mast.

It was a perfect starlight evening. Very romantic . . .

I wanted the world to stop at that moment. All my problems had ceased to exist, and life had acquired an illusion of perfection under the moonlight.

Sam was also in a reflective mood.

"Life never deals you the hand you expect, does it?" he asked, breaking the comfortable silence that had enveloped us.

I glanced at him.

"No, I don't suppose it does."

"I always thought I'd marry, have kids, spend my entire working life in the Navy and then retire."

He sighed. "Instead, what happens? I'm on the wrong side of forty and have a daughter I didn't know about for fifteen years . . . And then, the Navy cuts short my contract."

"At least you've seen something of the world," I pointed out. "And at least you know your daughter now. I'm alone. No ties . . ."

We were both silent for a moment, and then Sam looked at me.

"Well, we've both still got time to do something. Take a tilt at some rainbows . . . Live out our dreams."

"But first I've got to find another job," I interjected, ever practical.

"No, Anna." Sam looked at me and shook his head. "It's time for dreams. Do what you want to do before it really is too late."

The problem was, as I tried to explain to Sam, I didn't have a clue what I really, *really* wanted to do. I'd been in my rut too long. Now I was frightened of getting out of it.

He was silent for a moment, regarding me steadily.

"I set sail next week for the Med. I need a crew. Fancy a trip? It would give you a break to think, sort yourself out."

I was flattered, nervous, excited . . . scared.

"Wouldn't I be pretty pathetic as a crew? I've only ever done day sailing. I can't even navigate," I finished feebly.

"You've got the basic sailing know-how and you'd soon master navigation." Sam shrugged. "You can be chief cook and galley slave!"

I looked at him, longing just to say "yes" and forget the consequences.

"Can I think about it?" I said instead.

"Of course. Come on, the tide's on the turn. We need to get going."

That night, after walking me back to the cottage, Sam kissed me goodnight.

Lincoln

ALTHOUGH it is a cathedral city, Lincoln possesses all the old-world charm of a village. It is also steeped in history. Roman high galleys and Viking longboats were once moored on the quayside.

In the 15th century, Lincoln was a noteworthy and prosperous town, with its busy port and thriving wool trade. The Norman High Bridge (pictured), which spans the River Witham, is another link to the past.

From its magnificent cathedral, high on a hilltop, to its bustling cobbled streets and lovely black and white buildings, the city's rich history is on display for all to see and enjoy.

LINCOLN: J CAMPBELL KERR

"Think about my offer, Anna. There'll be no strings, no expectations. But I think we'll get along, and it's time you took a tilt at some of those rainbows."

I DIDN'T see Sam for the next couple of days. I was busy doing extra work at the café, clearing things out and cleaning the place now that it was closed.

I guessed Sam was busy preparing for his trip. But all the time his offer was on my mind. Part of me wanted to take this leap into the dark. But another part of me urged caution . . .

I finished work on Saturday evening, collected my last pay cheque and took a detour past the *Lovely Lady* on my way home. Perhaps Sam would be on board.

But, disappointingly, there was no sign of Sam anywhere, although the boat positively gleamed in the evening sun.

Sunday at home was quiet. I cleaned the cottage then cooked lunch. Afterwards, I went for a walk. The *Lovely Lady* was bobbing up and down on her mooring but there was still no sign of Sam.

A black-headed seagull suddenly screeched at me from the top of the tall mast on the *Lovely Lady* before turning away and flying off.

When I got back to the cottage there was a note from Sam pushed under the door. It was brief and to the point.

Sorry to miss you. I was hoping to say goodbye in person. It's been lovely meeting you, Anna. I do hope we meet up again. Best of luck in whatever direction life takes you — go tilt at some rainbows.

Take care, Sam.

PS. I sail on the morning tide on Tuesday, and I still need a galley slave.

I stifled a sigh of disappointment. It would have been nice to see him and have a last drink together before he set off. He made me feel good.

I didn't like admitting to myself how much I'd enjoyed that kiss . . .

Monday was a busy day for me. I'd made a long list of everything I could think of that would need doing if the cottage was going to be empty for a few months and slowly worked my way through it.

On Tuesday morning I was up bright and early, hauling my bulging bag down to the quay.

"Morning, Sam."

He glanced up at me, taking in the bag at my feet. A delighted smile crossed his face.

"Your cook reporting for duty, Cap'n," I said shyly.

"Welcome aboard. You'd better get your things stowed down below. We cast off in ten minutes."

Standing in the *Lovely Lady's* cockpit with Sam's arm around me as we motored out of the harbour, I knew I'd never forget the time I was made redundant. It was when my ship came in and set sail — with me on it. ❏

ROSALIE dipped her window-cleaning brush into the bucket of soapy water. She was pleased with her progress so far. She'd been up earlier than usual that morning, hoping to be well ahead when George left for work.

"You don't need to spring-clean," he'd said, giving her a kiss and a comforting squeeze. "The house is fine."

"I'll feel better when I've given the place a good going-over," Rosalie had replied, though she knew her smile was forced. When he'd gone, she'd had to wipe her eyes briskly.

"Stop it," she'd told herself sternly. She'd made herself sing along with a silly song on the radio while she washed the dishes, and then, before she could feel mopey again, she got busy in the living-room. She shifted all the moveable furniture and poked the vacuum cleaner

by Judith Davis

Look To The Future

Illustration by David Young.

nozzle down behind the other pieces so that soon every vestige of dust — and a few unwary spiders — had been cleared away.

Next, she cleaned the insides of the living-room windows, staring out at the blue-grey sky, into which, only yesterday, Diana had disappeared, flying off to college for another term.

It wasn't the first time she'd seen one of her children off. For goodness' sake, James and Peter had left home, three and five years before. It was just that Diana was the youngest. The last to go.

Last October, when Diana had started college, Rosalie had felt excited, anticipating a new life opening up for herself and George, without the family. But nothing much had changed, and she'd found herself counting the days till Christmas, when they'd return. That had passed all too quickly, in a jolly, festive blur.

At Easter, only Diana had visited. It had been lovely having her, and Rosalie didn't begrudge her sons their impromptu holiday with their girl-friends to a sunny destination. It was natural that they should break away. But she did miss them . . .

For so long, she and George had been wrapped up in their children's lives, their schooling, their friends, their progress, their problems. Now, it was as if the two of them had been left behind. Despite trying to feel generous towards her offspring, Rosalie was ashamed to say that she felt slightly envious of their new lives.

As she rubbed at the glass she felt herself flushing. What an admission! Imagine being jealous of your own children. She rubbed harder and became aware that her friend, Milly, from Number Six, was walking past. Rosalie waved her duster, wishing she could have hidden her flushed face behind the net curtains, but they were already rinsed and out on the line.

SHE pushed the furniture back and surveyed the result. Yes, that looked better. But she wasn't finished yet. She pulled the vacuum cleaner along the hallway and into Diana's bedroom.

Rosalie hurriedly vacuumed and polished, emptying the bin and wiping talcum powder from the dressing table while trying not to notice all the reminders of Diana's childhood. She missed her daughter most of all, though she wouldn't admit it.

After that, Rosalie filled a bucket and pulled on her coat. Outside, the fresh breeze made her shiver and the dancing tulips beneath the apple tree were a cheerful reminder that spring was well under way.

She felt better out of the house. For the past two weeks, every room had hummed with Diana's lively personality, and had been littered with her scattered books and belongings. Yesterday, there had been a frantic rush to get everything collected after breakfast.

Then George had started fussing about the time and they'd had to rush to the airport, where, after checking in, Diana had suddenly gone

114

quiet, with that tense, pre-parting look on her face. Rosalie had known she'd looked the same.

George had charged off to the news stand to buy Diana some magazines, while Rosalie chatted about anything and everything, until the flight was called. Then she'd pulled Diana into a hurried hug during which they both tried not to cry.

George had put his arm around her while their daughter walked away through the departure gate towards another three-month term. She wouldn't be home in the summer for long — she was studying archaeology and would be spending six weeks of the summer break on a dig.

ROSALIE splashed more water on to the windows, scrubbing crossly at a smear. She'd never been on anything as interesting as an archaeological dig. She had left school at sixteen and worked in an office until her marriage, and then she'd continued working until the imminent arrival of her first child.

"Young people have so many opportunities nowadays," she muttered huffily to herself.

The sound of seagulls overhead made Rosalie glare upwards.

"Don't you dare drop any offerings on my clean net curtains," she muttered, shaking her brush at them.

They passed, gliding on white wings, towards their cliffside nests on the coast less than half a mile away.

The windows still looked smeary. Rosalie tutted. She'd never been much good at cleaning windows. George usually got the hose out to rinse them, but Rosalie didn't like using it. It always seemed to squirt all over the place, and it was such a bother getting it untangled.

She put the brush back in her bucket and straightened up as her back gave a twinge. Rain was forecast, and a north-easterly gale, which would tear across the Irish Sea and, no doubt, coat the windows with salt. What was she fussing for?

Even as she thought this, Rosalie felt a few raindrops on her face. Hurriedly she headed for the back door. Now, what about that washing? Should she bring it in, or not?

A sudden strong gust of wind and a scatter of heavier raindrops made up her mind. She grabbed the peg bag and ran towards the washing line.

By the time she had returned indoors she was as wet as the newly-washed net curtains. She hung them on the airer and decided to have a coffee break. As she took a mug from the rack the doorbell rang.

"Hi," Milly said, when Rosalie opened the door. "I've brought us an elevenses treat. I thought you'd need cheering up."

"Oh, Milly," Rosalie said. "How nice. Come on in. I've got the kettle on."

Milly set two fat eccles cakes on plates. She knew her way around Rosalie's kitchen as well as Rosalie knew hers.

"Did Diana get back to college OK?" she asked.

"Yes, she rang last night. She sounded fine — glad to get back to her mates and all that." Rosalie filled the mugs and put the milk jug and sugar basin on the table. Milly was always trying to lose weight, but she still liked her coffee sweet.

"Milly, does it ever get any easier?" Rosalie asked, when a few mouthfuls of the eccles cake had made her slightly more cheerful.

"Not so as you'd notice," Milly said. "My lot haven't been home for three years."

"Oh, Milly!" Rosalie felt mean for complaining. Milly's family was older than hers, and they'd all left the Isle of Man for good. Her two sons were settled in England and her daughter was teaching in Australia.

"Not that we don't keep in touch." Milly grinned. "Our phone bill is enormous. And, of course, you know we visit the boys at least once a year. But I've got something to tell you. We've only just decided!" Milly wriggled in her seat excitedly. "We thought we might visit Denise next winter — it will be summer-time in Australia and she'll be on holiday."

"Oh, Milly, that's wonderful." Rosalie knew how much Milly missed her only daughter, and she was often thankful that at least her family was only a short ferry or plane trip away.

"Claude thinks we should go, before we get past it."

Milly giggled, and Rosalie joined in, though after Milly had rushed off and she was rinsing the mugs, she didn't feel quite so cheerful. Milly wasn't much older than she was.

The chiming of the clock made her look up.

Good gracious, the morning had slipped past and she hadn't even made her sandwich for lunch. It was almost time to get ready for work.

Rosalie had a part-time job in an estate agent's office. She'd been very nervous when she'd started, but now her job was a way of life and, lately, had been more important than ever in keeping her busy.

"Stops me moping," she reminded herself sternly, as she selected a jacket and skirt from the wardrobe and found a clean blouse. "And where would we have been without my wages?"

As she drove to work Rosalie couldn't help thinking again about the future. She must fill this gap that the children had left, but with what?

116

She had to consider George, too. He worked flexible hours, and he liked her to be around. But if they had a little more cash they could afford to go and see their family more often . . .

A busy afternoon made family thoughts flee and, by the time she was driving home again, Rosalie felt calmer and slightly more like her usual optimistic self. The worst of the parting ache was fading now, as it always did, after twenty-four hours.

Between tasks that afternoon she had kept reminding herself that now they were on their own, they could enjoy the peace and quiet.

For a start, she and George could watch what they wanted on TV without argument or embarrassment. They both liked the sort of programmes that the children regarded as "old hat".

The house would stay tidy, the washing machine unpressured, the bathroom neat. Food planned for the week's meals would remain in the fridge until needed, instead of being used up in some late-night curry which would smell the house out for days and usually result in some item of crockery or cookware being irreparably burned or broken.

ROSALIE drew up at the gate and battled her way from the car through the rain and driving wind, trying her very best to keep hold of these fragile consolations. But, as she pushed her key into the lock, she knew that she would give up any amount of TV programmes and overlook any mess if it were possible to recapture those wonderful family years which had now gone for ever.

She almost fell into the hall and pushed the door shut behind her.

"George? Are you back, love?"

George emerged from the living-room, grinning.

"Yes, and glad to see you." He put his arms about her. "Are you feeling better?"

"Oh, George!" Rosalie hugged him. "You knew how I was feeling, didn't you?"

"I know when you get that spring-cleaning urge you're fed up."

"Is it that obvious?"

"Yes," George said. "But come on in. You've got a surprise."

"What? Oh, George!"

George swung open the living-room door. He'd drawn the curtains against the driving rain and had switched on the wall lights and the shaded lamps with their warm orange glow. But it wasn't their cheeriness that made Rosalie gasp — it was the beautiful bouquet of flowers that immediately lifted her spirits.

"They're gorgeous!" she said. "Oh, and they're scented. What a wonderful smell. George, you shouldn't have."

"I didn't," George said. "The family did."

He handed her a florist's card with a message written in Diana's unmistakable hand.

"She must have arranged for them to be delivered."

Rosalie felt tears coming to her eyes.

"*To Mum and Dad,*" she read aloud, "*with all our love and thanks for everything.*" She looked up at George. "And it's from the three of them."

"But I reckon it would be Diana's idea. She's a thoughtful girl," George said. "We've brought her up well."

Rosalie fumbled for a hanky.

"Oh, George, isn't that nice? And, oh, I've got something to tell you. I've asked if I can try full-time work for a while. It will mean a rise in wages. What do you think?"

"I think that's great, love."

"You don't mind if I'm not always here when you are?"

"Not at all. I'll maybe get a few jobs done about the house that I've been meaning to do for years."

"Oh, George." Rosalie fingered one of the delicate flowers. "Shall we open a bottle of wine with our meal tonight? I think we've both got something to celebrate."

"Have we?"

"Yes." Rosalie took his hand. "I think we should celebrate the fact that we've got through our family years with flying colours." She felt George's fingers squeezing hers.

"And now perhaps it's time to look to our own lives again. We've had a lovely time with the children, but we've got a great many years still ahead of us."

"I hope so," George said, trying not to smile.

"No, listen. It's true, what you said. I think we have brought Diana up well, and the boys, too. And the fact that we don't see them much won't alter that.

"As long as we keep in touch and let them know we still care, and we're here if they need us, that's what matters. Who knows, perhaps one day one of them might return to the island to raise a family of their own."

George put his arm about Rosalie's shoulders.

"I knew I did the right thing, marrying you, all those years ago."

"Oh, George." Rosalie beamed. "Just think of all the things we might do in the future."

"Well," George pondered. "I can't think of any at present, but you're right. We've got a freedom now that we haven't had for years."

"So, do you agree? We should think ourselves lucky?"

George knew that Rosalie had assumed some of this optimism, but he also realised that what she was saying was true. Children are wonderful, but they weren't the be all and end all. He and Rosalie were that.

"So," he said. "You'll not go mad, spring cleaning after the next family visit?"

"I'll not promise." Rosalie smiled. "We have to be realistic. But I'll try, yes. I'll certainly try." ❏

by
Eleanor
Neville

Illustration by Sally Rowe.

TAKING THE PLUNGE

I DO think you're brave," Sue said, and Steve began to feel a little better.

The sensation only lasted seconds, because Tony, who occupied a desk on the other side of the office without doing anything useful, sniggered.

"What sort of idiot jumps off the side of a building on the end of a bit of string to raise cash for charity?"

That was a question Steve had been asking himself since he'd volunteered — with a small refinement. His question was, what sort of idiot who's scared of heights would jump off the side of a building for *any* reason?

Above Crovie, Aberdeenshire.

Abseiling wasn't the same as jumping, of course, and if children in Romanian orphanages weren't a good cause then he didn't know what was.

But he still didn't know why he'd said he'd do it or even if he'd be able to go through with it — and he definitely didn't have a clever answer for Tony.

Luckily, he had Sue, who'd never been lost for words in her life, as far as he could see.

"Because he's the sort of bloke who cares about something other than himself!" she said fiercely, and Steve tried to look suitably modest.

"He's nuts," Tony said dismissively, and Steve wondered which of them was right.

He forced himself to get on with his work, while keeping a look-out for anyone who came into the vicinity. If he was risking life and limb, the least people could do was sponsor him.

So why had he agreed to do it? Not to appeal to girls — at least, he hoped that wasn't the reason. True, Sue had been there when he'd volunteered, but he hadn't fancied her then. He didn't really fancy her now, but he couldn't help noticing the way the sunlight glinted on her hair, turning it to chestnut, or how her eyes shone when she smiled, or when she was cross.

She was cross quite often, because she didn't suffer fools gladly. But she was also his boss, which considerably limited the opportunities for romance. He wasn't, to use a cliché, that sort of boy.

Then again, he'd never thought of himself as the sort of boy who leaped blithely off tall buildings, either.

At pushing thirty, he wasn't exactly a boy anyway. He was, as Sue had put it, a bloke. He'd had his fair share of relationships, but so far had managed to avoid matrimony. Two years on an oil rig and two more in Saudi Arabia had helped there, but it was hard picking up the threads of your life after being away for so long.

Was that why he was doing it he wondered, as he headed for the sandwich bar at lunchtime. As a way of improving his social life? It was

After The Harvest

NOW the year is slowing down,
Nature seems to take a breath.
Woodlands turn to russet brown,
Mists enfold the purple heath.

Ripened fruits lie under eaves,
Roses' velvet petals spill,
Bonfires burn the fallen leaves,
Sheep are gathered from the hill.

Mountain peaks wear caps of white,
Icy winds come all too soon,
Stubble fields are ghostly-bright
Under an enormous moon.

Southward now the swallow flies,
Squirrels hoard against the cold.
Fires are lit as summer dies
In a blaze of red and gold.
— *Brenda G. Macrow.*

I. Robertson.

a bit drastic if it was.

He didn't think it was. He was doing it because . . . because the pictures of those kids had gone straight to his heart, completely by-passing his brain.

And now he was scared, but he wasn't backing out. For one thing, he'd collected all those sponsors on his sheet, and for another, he'd be letting down those kids. And, lastly — which shouldn't have been the most important to him, but was — what sort of wimp reached thirty and was still afraid of heights?

No, that wasn't quite true. Heights he was fine about. It was the falling and hitting the ground and breaking every bone in his body he was afraid of. So what was he doing, planning to jump off the edge of a building attached to a long piece of string, as Tony had put it?

"You're quiet," Sue said as he joined him in the lift and the doors closed. He tried to smile, glad of any distraction from the thought of hurtling towards the concrete attached to a rope.

"Was I? Sorry."

"Is Tony getting to you?" she asked.

He realised she knew he was worried, so he gave up on fake smiles and settled for what he hoped was a manly shrug.

"He's just jealous because he hasn't got the guts." Her hand rested on his arm for a second. He suspected it was supposed to be comforting, but it was no help at all really, because it left Steve even less sure that he'd got the necessary guts.

"Not like you," Sue went on as they headed out of the office and down the street.

"Do you want me to come and watch?"

That wasn't a bad idea, he realised. He couldn't talk to her properly in the office where she was the boss, and he wasn't sure she'd noticed him any more than she'd noticed the photocopier. But seeing him out of work — assuming he didn't make a fool of himself — was a different matter.

"Won't you be busy?" What he really wanted to ask was, "Have you got a boyfriend?"

"Me?" She pulled a face, and Steve lost a little more of his heart.

"The highlight of my weekend is going to be mowing the lawn. But won't you have loads of people there to cheer you on?"

Was that the reverse of his question, of just a polite query? Still, at least worrying about that was better than worrying about jumping off that building.

"It's a very select gathering." He grinned. "One — and you'd be it."

"Ah," she said, which was no help either.

He hadn't a clue whether that was an "ah, good, there's a vacancy I could fill", an "ah, so you're a sad loser who hasn't got a girlfriend", or just an "ah, I'm not sure what else to say".

Luckily, they reached the sandwich bar, and he knew what he was doing there. He ordered tuna and mayonnaise, and tried not to wonder what he'd look like when they scraped him off the pavement.

"When is it scheduled?" she asked as they walked back together.

"Half past ten, Saturday morning," he said, managing to suppress a shudder.

He felt better knowing she was going to be there cheering him on — until he realised it meant there was no way he could chicken out now.

SATURDAY morning dawned bright and clear, a perfect day for abseiling — so that was another excuse gone. Steve stared at his reflection while he shaved, acknowledging that he was not looking his best. The dark rings round his eyes bore testimony to a night that had been roughly evenly split between nightmares and lying awake.

He tried desperately to think about something nice. Sue was the first thing that came to mind, and he imagined gliding gracefully down the building and landing at her feet. She'd fling her arms round his neck and say how brave he'd been . . .

Who was he trying to kid? She wasn't going to see him as a hero, because he wasn't one!

Heroes weren't scared. You never saw James Bond deciding to skip breakfast in case he threw up, did you? Or Indiana Jones?

OK, they were both fictional characters, but the point was just as valid. He wasn't a hero. He was a scared wimp, about to make the biggest mistake of his life.

"Maybe not." He gave himself a pep talk because there was no-one else to do it.

"I'm not thirty yet. There are much bigger mistakes waiting for me out there!"

Like asking Sue out, and being turned down and wrecking both a friendship and an office relationship. He thought she liked him, and they certainly always seemed to go to lunch at the same time, although some of those coincidences were down to careful organisation on his part.

Some, he hoped, were down to her, but what if they weren't? What if she was just joining him for the sake of company morale, or, worse still, because she felt sorry for him? What if he made a real fool of himself?

"Idiot!" He went back to the pep-talk.

"You think you've got problems? What about those kids in that orphanage? Not enough to eat, no clothes, not even a Teddy bear!"

It was a good point, and just what he needed to spur him on.

He drank one cup of black coffee, then headed off to the tall office building he was to abseil down. It seemed to have grown at least five extra storeys since the night before. It loomed, large and ominous, against the cloudless sky, and even the sight of Sue waiting at the front door couldn't help.

"I couldn't do this," she said in an awed voice as he joined her, both of them staring up . . . and up . . . and up . . .

"I'm not exactly happy about it myself," he admitted.

He didn't want to be there any longer, because it was too easy to think about chickening out, so he made his way to the top of the building, reflecting grimly on how much quicker the downward journey was going to be. He was met at the top by a group of people, none of whom looked any more enthusiastic than he felt.

He could hear mutterings all around him, and the general tone of them was, "How did I get myself into this?" which caused the first real grin of the day.

He might be a coward, but he was in good company. He picked a spot between two burly blokes who looked as if they knew what they were doing. He realised, however, as they got their safety harnesses in a tangle, that you shouldn't judge by appearances.

"Your first time?" he asked as he helped untangle them, glad of someone to talk to.

Local Hero

IMAGES from "Local Hero" (1983) remain in the hearts and memories of those who have seen it long after the film-makers packed up and left the sleepy fishing village of Pennan, known in the film as Ferness.

The well-loved film, which was directed by Bill Forsyth, is still drawing people to the Aberdeenshire village today, following in the footsteps of the oil executives of the story — played by Burt Lancaster and Peter Riegert — who want to buy the village to make way for a refinery.

The executives encounter considerable resistance from the assortment of local eccentrics and eventually scrap their plans, enchanted by the quirky people and beauty of their surroundings. Lancaster's character — a keen astronomer — decides instead to construct an observatory.

It's easy to see why Pennan captured the hearts of these characters and countless fans o the movie. It's a picturesque village, set below dramatic red sandstone cliffs, with a pebble beach which runs down to the

Pennan.

Tom Parker.

On The Silver Screen

"Yeah." The larger, burlier one looked distinctly green. "And . . ."

"The only way down is over the side," the organiser said gleefully, and Steve glared at him.

"I wonder if he'd bounce?" he muttered, and got a grin from his new mates.

"Worth a try. Oh, I wish . . ."

"I know." Now he'd got company, Steve could admit he was scared. "I don't even know why I'm doing it."

He wasn't alone in that, but that wasn't much help. He still had to put the harness on and step over the side of the building. But there was no turning back now.

"For the kids — for Sue — but most of all — for me," he muttered, then stepped out into space. This was it, the moment when he'd plunge to his death. But he didn't! He just hung there, like a conker on a piece of ea. Once upon a time, fishing was not the only industry here. The smuggling of liquor and silk was a lucrative business, too, thanks to the village's secret coves and caves.

Other scenes were shot at Camusdarrach in Morar — which is actually on the west coast of Scotland — to complete the illusion of the perfect Scottish coastal village. The beach house owned by Fulton Mackay's character in the film is actually located on the opposite side of the country, just south of Morar.

Dennis Hardley.

Camusdarrach.

Peter Capaldi and Burt Lancaster.

Perhaps the most lasting image of "Local Hero" is the red telephone box, which plays an important part in some of the film's crucial moments. While red telephone boxes have become something of a rarity round the country, being replaced with a modern design, a preservation order has been granted on Pennan's famous red box. A decision which movie-lovers the world over would approve of!

string, before he remembered what he'd been taught, and began to move carefully downwards.

By the time he reached the tenth floor, the initial fear had gone, replaced by grim resolution. By the time he reached the fifth floor and could make out Sue's face, strained and anxious, he was starting to consider enjoying himself.

And when, unbelievably soon after that, his feet touched solid ground and Sue's arms went round his neck before he could disentangle himself from the harness, he was definitely enjoying himself.

"You were incredible!" she said, and he shrugged in what he hoped was a modest fashion.

"It was for a good cause."

But he had been a hero in a way, which gave him just enough courage to take an even bigger risk. And that paid off, too — because she said yes! ❏

125

A Tou

by Vicky Taylor

"L ET'S sit down," Arthur said as they went into the crowded shopping centre. "We'll listen to the band for a bit, because you've worn me out, young Toby."

The Salvation Army, their uniforms a splash of red and blue, their instruments gleaming, were in

126

full flow. Arthur smiled as he watched them and remembered.

"Grandad!" an insistent voice said, and his smile was diverted to his grandson. Toby was only four, yet so full of questions that you'd think he'd burst if he didn't get them answered. They were good questions, too, and always set

h Of Magic

Illustration by Heidi Spindler.

"How will Father Christmas deliver the presents when our new house doesn't have a chimney?"

"Ah," Arthur said, to buy himself time. "What does your dad say?"

"He said I should ask you!"

Thanks, George, Arthur thought ruefully. Then he caught sight of a girl by the band, and the memories swamped him.

"I'd have to think about that for a bit. But I can tell you about the year he couldn't get down our chimney, if you like?"

"Yeah!" Toby's legs ached as much as Grandad's. He was only too happy to sit and listen while the carols played and the decorations glinted around them.

Grandad's stories about long-ago, when he'd been a boy, were the best.

"It must have been 1929, maybe 1930," Arthur began, conjuring up that long-ago time before central heating and supermarkets and everyone having a car. "I was four or five, and our house had a chimney, all right."

There wasn't often a fire in the fireplace beneath it, and never one upstairs unless someone was ill — but they had had a chimney. He'd been as excited then as young Toby was now about Christmas, so he'd asked his mam what she thought Father Christmas would bring, then wished he hadn't.

Arthur thinking, even if, sometimes, he didn't know the answers.

"What?" he asked, hoping that it wouldn't be another one along the lines of "Where does God live?"

127

"She looked really sad, you see," he explained. "And then she told me Father Christmas might not be able to come that year.

"I said she was talking nonsense, because Father Christmas always came, but she explained we hadn't been able to afford to have the chimney swept, so Father Christmas wouldn't be able to come down it. Safety regulations, you see.

"He could start a fire, or mess up the whole kitchen, and as to what it would do to his red outfit — well, Mother Christmas wouldn't stand for it. We didn't have washing machines back then . . ."

"Oh, Grandad!" Judging by his wide eyes, Toby understood the enormity of the disaster.

"Yes, I was really disappointed. Not that we got much for Christmas in those days; not like you spoiled lot today." He ruffled Toby's hair to take the sting out of the words.

"But it was meant to be a special day, a magic day, and now it wasn't going to be, and I went off to church in a really bad mood . . ."

Children went to church and Sunday School whether or not they wanted to, then. And in those long-ago days, children hadn't argued with their parents.

Not that he would have argued too much about Sunday School anyway, Arthur recalled. For one thing, the church hall was warm, and for another, he liked his teacher.

Miss Stuart was tall and fair and kind. She also stood for no nonsense, and she could see through brick walls; especially when one of her flock had been up to no good.

"What's up, Arthur?" she'd asked as the other children streamed outside to play.

"Nothing, Miss." He might be young, but he had his pride. There was no way he was admitting that, with Dad out of work, they hadn't the money to have the chimney swept, so Father Christmas couldn't come.

"Nothing?" she'd asked gently. "Then where's your Christmas smile?"

"Not going to be a proper Christmas, is it?" he'd retorted.

"Come on, tell me the worst. Maybe I can help?"

And so he'd let it all spill out; how unfair it was, how rotten Christmas was going to be, and how he couldn't say any of this to Mam or Dad, because they were miserable enough already.

They tried to hide it, just as he was pretending everything was all right, but there was no Christmas spirit in the house at all, and precious little money, either.

"And back then —" Arthur came back to the present long enough to explain to Toby "— that meant not enough cash for proper food or heating. If you scuffed your shoes, or ripped your shirt, then it was really serious."

"What happened then?" Toby asked.

"Nothing at first. Did I say it was a week before Christmas that all this happened? Well, it was, and I went home feeling a bit better because I'd told someone, and guilty because I'd blabbed secrets.

"When Miss Stuart came round a few days later, I wished I hadn't said anything at all . . ."

* * * *

"Mrs Moore?" she'd said quietly, almost as if she was nervous. "Could I come in for a while?"

"What's Arthur done?" his mam had asked, glaring at him in advance.

"What had you done?" Toby interrupted excitedly, and Arthur grinned.

"Can't remember." He could, and it had involved Susan Smith's pigtails being tied to the back of the chair — or had it been spiders down her neck? But Toby could cause quite enough chaos without lessons from his old grandad. Amnesia was the safest bet.

"Anyway, Mam wasn't best pleased with me, and she sent me away.

"Now, the house wasn't very big, and it was cold outside. Might even have been about to snow. It did snow at Christmas back then, so I went outside the door and waited . . ."

"I don't know how to say this." Miss Stuart had sounded nervous, which was something he'd thought was impossible. "But I've been talking to Arthur and he's not happy."

"Why not?"

"It's about Christmas." Miss Stuart's voice had been so quiet that he could hardly hear it. "And how Father Christmas isn't coming."

"He won't be the only child who doesn't get a visit round here, will he?" Mam's bitter pride left Arthur wishing he'd kept his mouth shut. "Since the factory closed . . ."

"I know, but he's a good child and, well, the church . . ."

"I don't want no charity." Mam had sounded so cross that Arthur edged backwards.

"Charity?" Miss Stuart's voice rose. "Mrs Moore, remember what we're celebrating.

"When the baby was born in the stable because there was no room at the inn, was that charity? Or was that the innkeeper seeing someone who needed help and giving it, just as Mary and Joseph would have helped him if they could? 'Do this in memory of me,' that's what Jesus said when He grew up."

Normally Arthur would have dismissed all this, but he'd never heard Miss Stuart sound so firm. What she was saying had sounded so right that it had sneaked straight into his memory and engraved itself there.

"And when the Three Kings brought their gifts, did Mary say, 'Go away, I don't want charity?' Of course not; she said thank you, and gave on when she could."

"Gave on?" Mam had said slowly, and Arthur had known he wasn't the only one for whom this was a new idea.

"This year, you need a little help." Miss Stuart's voice was soft, and something about it had left Arthur wanting to cry without knowing why.

"Next year, by the Grace of God, it'll be better for us all, and you can help someone else who needs it.

"Please, Mrs Moore, let us help? Let us make it a good Christmas for Arthur, and his brothers and sisters. It won't be much, but . . ."

"I'll have to talk to his dad," Mam had said, then went to put the kettle on.

S O?" Toby asked, when Arthur came back to the present and stopped. "What about the chimney and Father Christmas? Was it swept?"

"No, it wasn't swept, but when I woke up on Christmas morning there was one of Mam's stockings at the foot of the bed, and in it . . ." He smiled at the memory of what had seemed such incredible riches.

"There was an orange in the toe, and a bar of chocolate; a penny one, which was a big bar back then, and a wooden engine. And there was a chicken for dinner, and a Christmas pudding and . . ."

"So Father Christmas came, even though the chimney wasn't swept?" Toby's eyes were wide again. "How did he get in?"

"How? I don't know." Arthur shook his head. "That's the thing about Christmas. Things don't happen how you expect, and often you don't understand at the time, but Father Christmas came all right.

"And I learned what Christmas spirit really meant that year."

The boy wouldn't understand. With any luck he'd never have to, but there was something Arthur had to do. He reached for his wallet and, shook out a handful of pound coins.

"Over there is a lass with a collection box. Go and pop those in for me, would you?"

He watched Toby scamper off, and smiled.

"Give on," Miss Stuart had said. She was long dead now, but he was still doing what she'd said, just as Mam and Dad had, once things had got better. Somewhere, because of it, Father Christmas would come to a child this year, too.

With any luck, that child, too, would give on when he could, making another link in a chain that went all the way back to that innkeeper Miss Stuart had talked about.

As he thought of that, he felt a lump in his throat, and a feeling of Christmas that warmed his heart.

Then he settled down to think about Toby's problem, and by the time his grandson scampered back, he'd got the answer.

"Thank you, Toby." Arthur smiled at him. "And as for Father Christmas, he can come in through the letter-box or the cat-flap. It's magic, you see."

Actually, Christmas could come anywhere there was a loving heart, but Toby was too young to understand that. Just as his grandad had been, the year Father Christmas almost hadn't come at all . . . ❏

T HE first thing Pru felt when she heard about the Old Boys' Reunion was pleasure. That quickly changed to unease . . . "There are about thirty coming. I remember you said a school was evacuated here during the war," her friend, Sylvie, went on, as they tidied up the Old Barn tearoom, which was in the grounds of the stately home where they worked part-time.

"Do you remember any of the boys?"

An image of one boy in particular flashed through Pru's mind — a boy she'd known very well indeed, and remembered just as clearly.

"Yes, I remember some of them." She smiled. She had no intention of telling Sylvie she'd fallen head over heels in love, or it would be all round the village!

"The school was near the Kent coast, so they were sent here to Hampshire. Some were quite young, and the older ones in their teens. We

It's Never Too Late

By Christine Shinwell

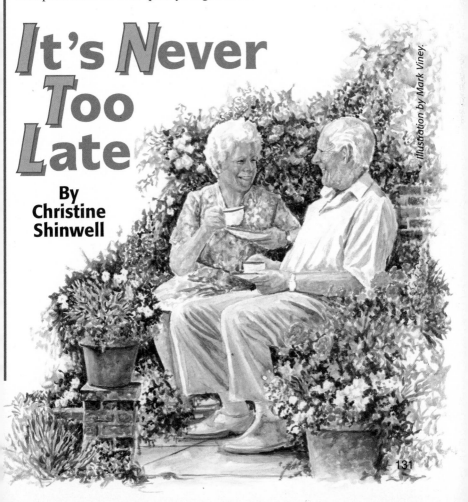

Illustration by Mark Viney.

didn't know what had hit us!"

"How old were you then?"

"Fourteen." As if she could forget.

"Oooooh, just old enough for romance." Sylvie grinned, and Pru turned away. "Some of them might even be on the look-out now. We might bag ourselves a rich widower!"

Pru had to laugh. At a mere sixty-eight, Sylvie's head was still filled with romantic notions. But Pru was far more sensible. Although she was a sprightly seventy-odd, she'd settled into widowhood some years back, when her beloved Dick had died after fifty years of happy marriage.

She had two children and four grandchildren. It was a pity they didn't live closer, so she could see more of them. But she had plenty of friends in the village, and the last thing she wanted was another man in her life.

And, more to the point, the last man she wanted to see was Hugh Marchant!

It was highly unlikely he'd be coming, anyway . . .

And, even if he did, he probably wouldn't recognise her. A lot of water had gone under the bridge since they'd last seen each other. He'd be too involved with his old chums to think about the naïve country girl he'd promised undying love to, then gone back home and forgotten . . .

Nevertheless, as Pru drifted off to sleep that evening, she felt it *might* be nice to see him again. Just out of curiosity . . .

SOME months later, as the newly arrived Old Boys strolled into the tearoom for morning coffee, Pru scanned their faces from behind the counter.

He wasn't there. Either that, or he'd changed beyond recognition!

She felt disappointed, but then pulled herself up sharply. What was she thinking about? She didn't want anything to do with Hugh Marchant!

*   *   *   *

"Hello, Pru."

The tearoom was empty, and Pru was clearing up, when she heard a voice behind her.

She swung round, and there he was — not unrecognisable at all, but still with the same smile, the same hazel eyes and the same little cleft in his chin that had made her teenage heart turn over.

"Hugh . . . I thought you weren't here," she said, immediately scolding herself for giving away the fact that she'd looked for him.

"I was late." He chuckled in a way she recalled so well. "Took the wrong turning and got lost. Remember how useless I was at finding my way around?"

She did, but she wasn't going to tell him that.

"I suppose you want some coffee?" she asked coolly, suddenly aware that Sylvie was gawping, boggle-eyed, from beyond the teapots.

"Yes, please," he answered, grinning sheepishly.

She remembered the effect that had had on her, too, but if he thought he could charm her like that again, he was mistaken!

"Thanks." He took the coffee. "Have you a few minutes to sit with me, just for old times' sake?"

He always was as bold as brass! She was about to say no, but then realised *that* would really give Sylvie something to gossip about.

"All right," she said grudgingly. "Just for a little while."

She poured herself a cup of coffee and led him out to the garden — away from prying eyes!

He still looked every inch the successful businessman's son, Pru decided — something she'd thought she could blithely ignore at a time when class distinctions were still a fact of life.

"I didn't expect to find you still here," he said, smiling. "Certainly not working in the tearoom!"

"It so happens I enjoy it."

What a cheek! As if she'd want to sit at home twiddling her thumbs all day!

"But don't you find it tiring, being on your feet for hours?" He spoke sincerely and Pru felt ashamed. After all, he was only here for the day. She should at least be polite, as she would with any old acquaintance.

Except he wasn't just an acquaintance. He was her first love — the person with whom she'd shared the first blossoming of heady romance.

"I like to keep active, and I enjoy the company," she replied, trying to sound more civil.

"Well, I must say, you look wonderful. Do you still live on the estate?"

"No, my husband and I had a cottage on a local farm, but we moved back to the village when we retired."

"And your husband . . .?" he asked hesitantly.

"Dick died five years ago. What about you?"

I bet he married someone educated and accomplished, she thought. Someone who was everything I wasn't . . .

"Grace passed away nearly three years ago. We were married for forty-seven years. I have a son, but he lives up north, so I don't see as much of him as I'd like. I took over my father's engineering business when he died, but I'm retired now and I moved to a village, still in Kent.

"The Hall hasn't change much," he went on. "Does the same family still own it?"

"Yes, but it's open to the public now, of course." Pru smiled. "Times have changed since the war."

"Are all those marble busts and formidable paintings we used to delight in mimicking still there?"

"Yes!" Pru couldn't help smiling as she recalled the fun they'd all had. Seeing the sedate place where her father was head gardener being invaded by hordes of boisterous schoolboys had been as exciting for her as it was for them.

Shielded from the realities of war, they'd been memorable years . . . except for the fact she'd landed up with a broken heart . . .

W ELL, I must be off." Pru got to her feet.

"Look, can we meet up again?" Hugh asked. "It's marvellous to be back. I decided to make a break of it and stay at the village pub for a few days, see some of the old haunts. Perhaps we could do some more reminiscing?"

"I don't know . . ." Pru hesitated. "I'm quite busy, what with the tearoom and so on . . ."

"Please, Pru." He smiled — that charming grin she'd never been able to resist. "I might never come here again. And we *did* have some good times together, didn't we?"

"Well, OK." She hadn't the heart to say no.

"Splendid! And now I'd better catch up with my old pals before they think I'm not coming."

She watched him walk out of the tearoom, a smartly dressed, distinguished-looking figure. It wasn't difficult to imagine how different their lives must have been. Then she thought of Dick, a farm worker all his life, and wondered how she could have imagined someone like Hugh would ever marry the gardener's daughter.

But that didn't excuse the way he'd treated her! He'd promised to write, sworn they'd see each other again, but she hadn't heard a word. Over the years she'd found it hard to forgive him.

"My word, he's a knockout, isn't he?" Sylvie had taken ten times as long as usual to clear up. "You're a sly one. Didn't let on that you'd had a teenage fling, did you?"

"It wasn't a fling." Pru sighed. "We were just friends, that's all."

"Oh, yes. So why's he making sheep's eyes at you, then?" Sylvie continued. "*And* he's staying on after the others have gone home."

"That's nothing to do with me!" Pru scoffed. "He just wants to revisit some old haunts, that's all."

But Sylvie wasn't finished.

"If you couldn't see how chuffed he was to see you," she said, folding her arms, "you're dafter than I thought!"

She's imagining things, Pru thought, as she walked home. He didn't want to see me *then*, so why should anything be different *now*?

That evening, she gave herself a stern talking-to. Sylvie was talking utter nonsense. She read too many romances, that was her trouble.

Hugh just wanted some company while he was here, Pru told herself. Then he'd go back home and she'd hear no more of him — just like last time.

Well, he wasn't going to get away with that again! It might be over half a century too late, but she could still teach him a lesson.

She'd go out with him just the once, and seem all sweetness and light. Then she'd tell him, quite politely, that he could jolly well find someone else to lead up the garden — or rather, the Hall — path.

She giggled, and suddenly remembered the very first time she'd seen him . . .

S HE was coming home from school, deliberately cutting through the Hall gardens in order to get a look at the boys who'd just arrived, when she came upon one of them.

He was edging along the branch of a tree near one of the drainpipes, egged on by a group of his friends. He looked down at her and grinned, hair tousled and shirt hanging out. And that was it. Pru fell in love on the spot.

"We had a bet on the date at the top of the drainpipe," he told her, and at that moment her heart had melted. "Whoever's nearest gets the biggest helping of pudding."

"It's 1520." Pru grinned back and giggled. "But if you get caught, you'll be for it."

With that, he clambered down and stood before her, hazel eyes sparkling and the cleft in his chin making her feel absurdly that she wanted to kiss it.

After that first meeting, there was no separating them. They wandered round the gardens, chatting about their very different lives, walked hand in hand through the woods, and shared their first, fumbling kisses in the pavilion.

Pru was walking on air. Her parents smiled indulgently, her schoolfriends were envious. She was gloriously, wondrously in love.

And the amazing thing was, he felt the same about her!

Time passed and Hugh soon turned fifteen.

Pru's parents were kept very busy with the war effort. Her father was in the Home Guard and had also taken over the home farm. Even the flower borders were full of vegetables!

KIBBLE PALACE, GLASGOW:
J CAMPBELL KERR

136

The local postman had gone off to war and her mother was delivering the area's post as well as being busier than ever in the Hall kitchens, now that there was a small army to feed.

"Hugh's a nice lad, but just remember the type of background he comes from, love," her mother warned. "He'll be going back home when he's sixteen. A life in a country village won't be for him."

It wouldn't be for either of them, Pru felt like protesting. Although she'd barely been out of her own neighbourhood, she'd led Hugh to believe she wouldn't mind living in the town where his father had his business. A business he'd be expected to take over eventually, something he dearly wanted to do.

As the dreaded sixteenth birthday approached, they talked of nothing else but their plans for the future. Pru happily concurred with anything Hugh suggested, whether she liked the sound of it or not. Their love was all that mattered.

"Once the war's over, we'll be together!" he told her.

The day he left she went to the station with him and waved until the train was just a speck in the distance.

"I'll write, as soon as I get home!" were the last words he called to her. "I love you, Pru!"

And that was the last she'd heard from him. It might have been only first love and their plans full of youthful optimism, but, oh, how she'd suffered because of him!

"You'll fall in love with someone else one day, you'll see," her mother had soothed. "Hugh will have had different expectations from you. You've years before you need to think about marriage. I know it seems awful now, but it'll pass and you'll forget him in time."

And, of course, she had, but nothing had ever hurt quite so much again.

In time, she'd realised it had been for the best. She'd married Dick, who came from a neighbouring village, and had been extremely happy. Her mother had been right — Hugh was from a different world.

The following day, Hugh asked her to lunch. Then they walked round the Hall, chatting away and often laughing over old times.

Kibble Palace, Glasgow

KIBBLE PALACE was the popular name given to a Winter Garden, originally built by John Kibble at his estate in Coulport, beside Loch Long. It was moved by raft down the Clyde to the city's Botanic Garden 1871, where it was then re-modelled on a grand scale.

This stunning dome-shaped glasshouse remains the garden's most impressive feature and, indeed, one of the finest structures in Glasgow itself. It's a must for all visitors to "the dear, green place".

After tea in the Old Barn tearoom — where Sylvie's eyes were nearly popping out of her head — they strolled around the gardens and down to the river. There they sat under the graceful old trees, as they'd done so often in the past.

But there was no holding hands this time, and he didn't mention their long-ago romance. It was as though it had never happened . . .

Nevertheless, Pru enjoyed herself, and when he suggested dinner she found it hard to refuse. Why go back to her empty cottage and eat alone, as she did most of the time?

She had to admit it was a lovely evening. They still got on well, and she could see why she'd been attracted to him all those years ago. It was a shame it had ended so bitterly, or she would have liked to keep in touch.

"Would you like to go to a pub for lunch tomorrow?" he asked, when they were about to say goodnight.

"I'm not sure," she hesitated. "I'm quite busy . . ."

"Please, Pru." He laughed. "You never used to hesitate."

"Well, what do you expect?" She glared at him, suddenly annoyed by his flippant tone. "Never a letter, not even a word, in all this time. All our promises just thrown overboard!"

"But . . . I *did* write." Hugh looked startled. "I wrote at least half a dozen times. There was no reply, so I just assumed you'd lost interest in me —"

"You *wrote* . . .?" Pru could hardly believe her ears. "But I never received any letters . . . Mother," she whispered as the penny dropped.

"You mean your mother intercepted them?"

"She must have! She used to deliver the post — remember?" Pru shook her head. "And she was a firm believer in people knowing their place."

"Oh, Pru . . . I know how much it hurt, because I felt it, too."

"She meant it for the best, I'm sure," Pru continued. "Probably thought that if we got married I'd be unhappy. She thought we were too young and would want different things out of life."

"Perhaps she was right." Hugh smiled sadly. "I mean . . . *would* it have worked?"

"I don't know." She thought of Dick and the love they'd shared. If it hadn't been for her mother, she wouldn't have had that. "But I don't regret it. It hurt terribly at the time, but I couldn't have wished for more happiness than I've had."

"I feel the same."

They smiled at each other, and then he took her hand.

"But I felt overjoyed when I found you here, Pru." Hugh tentatively reached out and took hold of her hand. "Do you think there's still time to carry on what we started? Romance isn't just for the young, is it?"

She squeezed his hand, loving the warmth of it, and felt a delightful urge to kiss the little cleft in his chin.

"No." She settled for his lips instead. "Sylvie's always saying you're never too old for romance. And now I think she's right!" ❏

by
Marion
Harris

APPLE BLOSSOM TIME

Illustration by
Melvyn Warren-Smith.

140

FAY PETERSON checked that baby Melanie had settled for her afternoon nap before carrying her mug of coffee out into the garden. She sat down on the wooden seat that stood in the sheltered corner of the patio and sighed, enjoying the peace and quiet.

It had been a long, hard winter, and she had begun to think spring would never arrive. Today, though, the sun was shining. It was mid-April, and the warmest day of the year so far, though Fay still needed her cosy cardigan.

What made the late spring doubly depressing was the fact that Daniel had been made redundant the week before Christmas. He'd applied for dozens of jobs since then, without any success — until last week, that was . . .

Fay sipped at her coffee and mentally crossed her fingers. With a little luck, Daniel would be successful at this interview and get the job he was after.

She'd been utterly convinced of this the moment she'd pulled back the bedroom curtains that morning, and had told him as much.

"I certainly hope you're right, but you shouldn't say things like that — it's tempting Fate," Daniel had warned, gathering her into his arms and kissing her gently.

"No," she'd insisted, "it's not! Look out the window — over there, at our apple tree. I'm sure it's in bud!"

"So it should be, at this time of the year." He'd grinned.

"Yes, I know that." Fay had smiled. "But everything in the garden is so late coming into flower this year. For the buds to appear overnight — well, that must mean something!"

Her voice had trailed away as she'd seen he was laughing at her. She hadn't minded, though. She knew he always teased her about her belief that everything good happened when the apple trees were in flower.

Now, sipping her mug of coffee, she thought about all the wonderful milestones in their lives that had occurred at this time of the year.

Four years ago, when she'd been just twenty, Daniel had proposed to her under the apple tree in her parents' garden — the very same spot where they'd first kissed a year before.

She remembered how the pink and white petals had suddenly showered down on to them, sticking to Daniel's thick dark hair like confetti.

They'd married the following spring, on a balmy day in April, with the sun so warm that they'd taken their champagne out into the garden. As they'd stood there, drinking a toast to each other, there had been apple blossom drifting on the breeze.

One of the things which had delighted Fay when they moved into their brand-new house was the apple tree in the garden. It looked almost as old as the one in her parents' garden.

It had belonged to the derelict mansion that had been demolished to make way for their new estate, and she'd been horrified when the builders wanted to chop it down. She'd insisted they left it alone.

The following year, in springtime, when the apple blossom was just appearing, their daughter had been born. And the year after that, Melanie had taken her first tottering steps, holding on to the gnarled trunk of the apple tree as the blossom floated down around her, carpeting the ground in pink and white.

That winter, in the severe November gales, the tree had blown over. To Fay, it was like losing a friend.

It was then that their luck seemed to change. The company Daniel worked for was bought over by a larger concern, and he was made redundant.

Fay's parents, worried about how they were going to manage, insisted that Daniel, Fay and Melanie should spend Christmas with them.

"Now, tell us what you'd like for Christmas, Fay," her parents had asked her. "This year, perhaps it should be something you really need, rather than a surprise present."

When Fay had asked for an apple tree they'd thought she was mad. She'd insisted that was what she wanted, however, and in the end they'd all gone along to the garden centre and selected one.

The tree hadn't been delivered until early spring and it was completely bare, with no sign of leaves or flower-buds.

"I'm not too sure if it will produce any fruit this year," the nurseryman had warned them. "It should have been in the ground long before this, but the weather has been too cold."

"Will it survive?" Fay had asked anxiously.

"It should do. Anyway, it's under guarantee," he'd reassured her. "If it doesn't come to anything, we'll replace it."

Fay had watched over it. Every morning when she'd drawn back the bedroom curtains, she'd looked out to see if there was any sign of leaves.

Gordon Henderson.

Golden Moment

WHEN, in a quiet time of recollection,
   I see the Cairngorms dressed in autumn gold —
The deep blue lochs that mirror their reflection,
Their forests like a blanket, fold on fold —
When I behold in dreams those soaring summits
Mantled in cloud, or white with early snow;
The shy red deer — a waterfall that plummets
From rocky height to purple glen below.

Then my heart lightens, though the year is ending.
The hills remain and cares are left behind
As, once again, I follow byways wending
Through russet woods — though only in the mind —
And see, above a hanging corrie high,
A golden eagle, circling on the sky.
                          — *Brenda G. Macrow.*

Loch Morlich.

The tree had stood, a bare outline against the cold sky, shaking in the chill spring winds.

Fay even talked to it sometimes, willing it to live. It meant so much to her and she was convinced they'd have a change of luck once it blossomed.

Then, like magic, the morning the letter arrived inviting Daniel to an interview, tiny, tightly packed, light-green leaves had appeared.

THE afternoon dragged by. Fay's mind was in turmoil and, as if sensing her mother's anxiety, Melanie couldn't settle, either. In the end, Fay took her outside. Hand in hand, they walked around the garden, counting the daffodils. Melanie touched each golden head repeating the number after her mother.

When Melanie tired of this game, they walked to the gate, watching for Daniel's return.

By now, the sun had dipped below the horizon and an east wind was chilling the air.

"Come on." Fay picked Melanie up in her arms. "It's time we went back indoors."

"No!" Melanie wriggled to free herself. "Daddy, Daddy!" she squealed, her podgy fingers pointing.

Fay's heart quickened as she saw Daniel walking along the road.

"What's happened?" she asked, concerned. "Where's the car?"

"It broke down, so I had to use the train." Daniel sighed. "I should have bought a new battery weeks ago, but I was afraid it would make too much of a hole in our bank balance."

He sounded so depressed that Fay was afraid to ask him about the job. She didn't feel she could take any more bad news.

As Melanie took his hand and dragged him off to look at the daffodils, Fay made her way indoors and switched on the kettle. She had a casserole in the oven, but that could wait until Melanie was in bed and they could sit down together.

She tried to shrug off her feeling of despondency as she poured the boiling water into the teapot. If *I* feel like this then think what Daniel must be going through, she told herself crossly.

"I see your lucky mascot is in flower at last," Daniel commented as he brought Melanie into the kitchen.

"Lucky mascot? I've a good mind to chop it down," Fay said heatedly.

"Don't do that." Daniel grinned. "It does work, after all."

For a moment, Fay didn't quite catch his meaning. Then, as she saw the smile that lit up his handsome face, her spirits soared.

"You mean . . .?"

"Yes!" he told her triumphantly. "I've got the job. Not quite as much money as I'd hoped, but there are plenty of prospects for promotion — probably about this time next year!" ❏

Four Little Words

C AN I come, too?"
That was all she'd asked. Who would have thought that four
innocent words could destroy a relationship?
She and Nick had seemed unbreakable. They'd had so much
fun together. They both loved pub quizzes — in fact, they'd met at one.
They both laughed at the same jokes, loved the same films, liked the
same music. They were both crazy about animals, too.

Lizzie had often thought that the main reason Nick was so keen to
accompany her to Sunday lunch with her parents had less to do with
her mother's brilliant cooking and everything to do with Sally, their
two-year-old Labrador.

Nick was kind, thoughtful and funny — and now he was gone.

What had she done? She sat curled up in her armchair, biting her
nails and wishing she'd never uttered that fatal question.

"Lizzie?" Nick had said when he'd phoned on Wednesday evening.
"Look, I'm really sorry, I can't come over tomorrow.

"My parents are coming down for a visit. They're staying at The
Grange and want to treat me to dinner."

"Dinner at The Grange? Lucky you!" Lizzie had laughed. "Can I

by Debby Holt

come, too?"

"Well, actually." Nick had sounded uncomfortable. "They did invite you, but I thought you'd probably find it boring. My dad's not the easiest of people to get along with."

"I'd really like to meet them." Lizzie paused. "Unless you'd rather I didn't."

"No, that's fine. I'll pick you up at eight."

The evening went badly from the beginning. Nick arrived punctually at eight, which was odd — he was never on time. Lizzie was still putting on her make-up and Nick could barely conceal his impatience. He wasn't acting like himself at all.

When they walked into the dining-room, Lizzie recognised his parents at once. His mother had Nick's curly chestnut hair and dark brown eyes.

"Nick!" she cried. "How lovely to see you! And you must be Lizzie. I'm Alice and this is Harry."

"It's good to meet you," Lizzie said. "Thank you for inviting me."

"We were beginning to think you weren't coming!" Harry Taylor glanced rather pointedly at his watch. "Never mind, you're here now. I thought I'd better go ahead and order, otherwise we'd be waiting all night. They tell me the chicken is very good.

"Are you happy with that?"

"Sounds lovely," Lizzie said politely. "I'm sorry we were late. That was my fault, I'm afraid."

"Women!" Harry gave a short laugh. "Never mind! So, Lizzie, I understand you've been seeing my son for some time."

"Yes, I suppose I have," she said as Harry poured the wine.

"Of course, Nick tells me you're not serious about each other, but it's nice to meet you all the same," Harry continued.

Lizzie tried to swallow the huge lump that had suddenly appeared in her throat. She nodded.

"Now, Nick, tell me about you." Harry turned to his son. "How's the job going?"

Lizzie barely spoke for the rest of the meal. Not that it seemed to matter, since Harry talked enough for everybody. Occasionally, his wife interjected with the odd comment or question, but her contributions were invariably overridden by Harry.

Nick did his best to bring the women into the conversation, but his efforts were like throwing sand in front of a steam-roller.

The meal seemed to drag on for ever. When Harry suggested coffee, Lizzie cleared her throat.

"Actually," she said, "I think I should go. I have an early start tomorrow."

Nick pushed back his chair.

"Don't get up, Nick, I can find my own way home," Lizzie told him quickly. "I'm sure you'd like to have some time with your parents.

"Thank you so much, Mr Taylor, Mrs Taylor. It was a lovely meal."

It was bliss to get out into the cool evening air — and a relief to let the

146

tears fall at last. She thrust her hands in her pockets and headed for home, hoping she wouldn't have to confront Nick until she was more composed. But when she turned into her road, he drove up beside her and leapt out of the car.

"Lizzie, I know you're upset!" he began. "It's what Dad said, isn't it? He only meant that we're not about to announce our engagement! You mustn't pay any attention to him. We're happy, aren't we?"

"We *were* happy." Lizzie took a deep breath. "I wish I hadn't come this evening. You didn't want me to, did you? Now I know why. Nick, I don't want to see you any more."

"Why?" Nick asked, clearly stunned. "What's changed?"

"Everything!" Lizzie felt tears well up in her eyes. "I don't mean I was hoping you would propose or anything. I just thought. I assumed it *was* serious between us. You clearly think otherwise.

"Please. I'm tired. Just leave me alone."

TWO weeks later, Lizzie was sitting in her parents' home on a warm Sunday afternoon, wondering if she'd ever stop feeling so alone. But it was good to be at home, to revel in the familiar smells of Sunday lunch, the enthusiasm of Sally's welcome, and the warm affection of her parents.

"Lizzie, be a love and lay the table, will you?" her mum said. "Your father's only got as far as taking the cutlery into the dining-room!"

"Right," Lizzie said, just as the dog decided she wanted some attention. "Sally, will you get down? When are you going to learn not to jump up at me? Yes, I love you, too, but these trousers are new!"

Lizzie was laughing as she went through to the dining-room. Then she stopped suddenly in the doorway when something outside the open window caught her eye. It was Nick.

"Lizzie," he said softly. "I want you to listen to me. You're not the only one who's been doing some thinking. I thought we were happy. I just never thought about *why* I was happy.

"Well, now I know. It's because I love you.

"I want to get married, Lizzie. I mean, I really, really want to get married."

Unsure at first, Lizzie moved cautiously to the window. But when she saw the look of love in Nick's eyes, she knew at once she wanted to spend the rest of her life with him.

She hurried out of the house and into the garden, where Nick stood, waiting miserably.

"Will you marry me?" he asked, his voice barely a whisper.

Four little words. Who would have thought four little words could change her life in an instant? Lizzie's eyes filled with tears, but she was smiling.

"Yes, please," she said, as Nick took her in his arms. ❏

I DON'T want a new year." Debbie's voice was wobbly. "Why can't we keep this one?"

"Don't be silly, Debs," her mother replied. "It's going to be a great year."

"And you'll have fun seeing it in with Granny and Grandad," her father added as the three of them walked towards her grandparents' house.

"How long do I have to stay with them?" Debbie asked, although she already knew the answer.

"We've told you, Princess, we're not really sure." Her father tried to take hold of her hand, but Debbie snatched it away.

"Just for a few days, while Mummy has your new baby brother.

"As soon as he's born, you'll be able to go and see them both. Of course, I'll be sleeping at Grandad's, too, so I'll be able to read your bedtime story."

Baby Talk

Debbie tried not to cry. She just knew that this had been her best year ever. She couldn't remember the others very well, but this year had been so full of lovely things, following one after another like shiny beads on a string . . .

First, there had been her birthday. That was when Daddy saw her in her floaty dress and began to call her his princess. She'd had a party, with proper games and a cake in the shape of a castle.

Easter had been a time of colourful boxes, with flowers and chicks on the outside and chocolate eggs inside. After Easter, she'd been old enough to go to playgroup.

She and her friend, Susan, had started on the same day. It had been scary for a little while, but they soon found plenty to do and enjoyed themselves.

That first morning, they had painted pictures which they were allowed to take home.

Debbie's mother had been so pleased with hers that she'd

taped it to the front of the fridge for Daddy to see when he came home from work.

There had been some bad things, too, like the time she tripped over and cut her knee so badly that she'd had to go to hospital.

Everybody had told her what a brave girl she was and the doctor had given her a badge which had *Well Done* printed on it.

Afterwards, she'd been allowed to stay up late and go to a burger bar and choose whatever she wanted to eat.

Illustration by Roberts.

by Sheena Groves

That pain had gone away quite quickly, but what she was feeling now was a different sort of hurt.

Summer had been hot with golden sunshine and big white birds crying as though they had sad and wonderful stories to tell. It had been a time of buckets and spades and ice-cream, and for paddling in the sea — that magical moving carpet of blue and green.

There had been so much to enjoy that she had hardly listened when her mother pulled her on to her lap one afternoon on the beach.

"Guess what, Debs?" Mummy had whispered. "You're going to have a baby brother or sister in a few months' time!"

A few months had sounded like for ever to Debbie and, in the meantime, she could see a lovely pink shell lying close by. Wriggling down, she ran to add it to her collection.

DEBBIE couldn't believe it when her father took her shopping one day to choose some paint for the room that he used as an office. "It's going to be your very own bedroom now, Princess."

"But I've got a room," Debbie had protested.

It was a small room which led off Mummy and Daddy's bedroom, but she felt safe and comfortable there. Her new room was the one along the passage where they might not even hear her if she woke in the night.

"It's time for you to have a big girl's room now, with your own furniture," her father told her. "You can choose curtains and pictures for it, and there will be lots more space for all your toys and books.

"Besides, we'll need the little room for the new baby."

Debbie thought this was a very bad idea.

"Do we have to have this baby?" she asked one day, but her mother just laughed.

"Darling, we *want* this baby. He, or she, is already with us, know you." She patted her tummy. "Tucked away inside here, growing big enough to come out and live in the world."

"Did I grow in your tummy?" Debbie was horrified.

"You certainly did," her mother said, putting her arms around her.

It was soon after that that her parents began to look worried. They would stop whatever they were saying when Debbie came into the room, and she could tell that they had been talking about the baby.

Debbie knew what they were thinking — that soon, they wouldn't want her around. They kept *telling* her that they would love her just as much, and that she would be a brilliant big sister. But, if that was true, why did they change the subject if anyone asked about the baby in front of her?

Suddenly, the baby became a "he". And "he" was going to be born in the new year. Mummy was going to go away for several days because the baby would be taken out of her tummy in the hospital, and Debbie would have to stay with Granny and Grandad.

150

Baby Talk

Perhaps the new year wouldn't happen, Debbie thought hopefully. And, then, along came Christmas.

Debbie was sleeping in her new room by then, and it wasn't as bad as she thought it would be. She hadn't wanted to choose the colours but, in the end, she simply had to.

"Right then, let's have dark brown with orange and purple stripes," her dad had said in the DIY shop.

Debbie had to do something to stop him, so she picked a pretty yellow for the walls and some curtains with daisies all over them.

Someone must have told Santa that she had moved to a different room because, on Christmas morning, a bulging pillowcase was tied to the foot of her new pine bed.

Debbie didn't think that anyone in the world could have had a more beautiful tree than theirs, with its red and silver ribbons and twinkling fairy lights. She ate grown-up dinner and Daddy lit a blue fire on the pudding, and then they pulled crackers and hers had a bracelet in it.

As they walked up the path to her grandparents' house, however, Debbie knew that everything was going to be different.

"I don't want a new year," she muttered again.

"What's that, pet?" her grandfather asked, swooping her up in his arms.

"She'll be all right, Dad," Debbie's father said, placing her little rucksack down in the hall.

He kissed her and then her mother leaned forward to kiss her, too. She seemed to have a cold because her eyes looked watery and her voice was quiet.

"'Bye, darling." She smiled. "Be a good girl for Granny and Grandad. Daddy will be back tonight and I'll see you very soon. And then you'll finally get to meet your brother!"

THANK goodness you're here, Debbie." Granny came out of the kitchen, wiping her hands on her apron. "I'm just baking a batch of gingerbread men and no-one can do the currant faces as well as you can. Come and give me a hand, sweetheart."

Debbie bit her lip. She supposed that this baby business wasn't really Granny's fault, so if she needed help it would be mean to say no.

She was surprised at how quickly the day went by. The gingerbread men looked delicious when they were cooked. Debbie picked out the one with the nicest face for her father to eat when he came back that night.

"When will Daddy come?" she asked over supper.

"I don't really know, love," her grandmother replied. "But you can stay up for a bit. After all, it is New Year's Eve."

Grandad put the television on and Debbie lay on the sofa with her thumb in her mouth. She knew that big girls shouldn't need their thumbs, but she didn't care.

Glen Nevis.

On The Silver Screen

Braveheart

IT'S certainly ironic that "Braveheart" (1995), one of the most famous Scottish films made in recent years, was mostly shot in Ireland.

The movie's producers were enticed away from the country of William Wallace's birth and life by the

Mel Gibson.

She must have fallen asleep because, the next time she looked at the TV, she saw lots of people enjoying a party, with streamers and balloons. Granny was just putting the phone down.

"I think you'd better go up to bed, darling. It doesn't look as if Daddy's going to be able to get back tonight." As she took Debbie's hand, all the people on the television began to shout "Happy New Year" to each other.

So that was it, Debbie thought. Of course Daddy wasn't coming back — they must have been planning it all the time! The new year had happened and Mummy and Daddy were going to leave her here and live at home with the baby.

When he was big enough he would probably even sleep in her new bedroom. She wished now that she had let it be painted orange and purple and brown!

Stiff and silent, she fought back tears as Granny undressed her and

152

merald Isle's promise of ocations more in keeping with he story's period.

Nevertheless, filming did at east *begin* in Scotland. A mediaeval village was constructed in Glen Nevis for he scenes where we see Wallace, played by Mel Gibson, woo and marry his sweetheart, played by Scottish actress Catherine McCormack.

Glen Nevis is a famous beauty spot, part of which orms the end of the famous West Highland Way. In fact, some would even go so far as o say that the Glen is Scotland's finest, with its waterfalls, woods and, of course, magnificent Ben Nevis, Britain's highest mountain.

The area has played host to its fair share of actors. Not long after the "Braveheart" crew left the area, the makers of "Rob Roy" appeared and constructed another village, this time representing life in the

Behind the scenes.

17th and early 18th centuries, under Ben Nevis.

From Glen Nevis, the story of Wallace's battle for his country's freedom moved to Ireland. Dunsoghly Castle near Dublin became Edinburgh Castle, while nearby Trim Castle was used as a backdrop to the London scenes.

Despite Scotland not having a starring role, the film still manages to capture the excitement and romance of the story of Braveheart — the archetypal Scottish hero.

pulled her nightie over her head.

"Don't worry, Debbie. Daddy will be here tomorrow," she said. But her face was serious, not smiley as it usually was. Granny was obviously feeling bad about her part in the plot . . .

DEBBIE hadn't expected to sleep at all in the little bed that had once been Daddy's, so she was surprised to find that it was already light when she was woken by Grandad.

"Jump up, pet!" he told her. "There's a call for you!"

No-one had ever telephoned her before!

Grandad helped her with her dressing-gown and slippers and she ran downstairs to where Granny was standing, holding out the receiver.

"Happy New Year, Debbie," Gran whispered. Debbie noticed that her smiley face was back.

"Congratulations, Princess!" Her daddy's voice echoed down the phone line. "You've got a baby brother and he looks just like you. He's longing to meet you, so I said we'd go in this afternoon after he and Mummy have had a rest.

"I'm on my way home now — please ask Granny to get the frying pan out, I'm starving!"

"We kept you a gingerbread man," Debbie told him.

"My favourite breakfast!" Daddy laughed. "Can I have him with eggs and bacon?"

When Daddy came in, Debbie was so pleased to see him that she forgot to be angry. Maybe it wouldn't be too bad living with Granny and Grandad if her parents came to visit quite often.

She tried not to think about the baby being in *her* room. Everyone seemed happy, so he must be something special — no wonder her parents preferred him to her.

Mummy was sitting up in bed in a room full of flowers. Next to her was a cot with a white bundle in it.

"Come and give me a big hug, Debbie," Mummy said, holding out her arms.

It was all too much for Debbie, feeling the close, comforting warmth of her mother and knowing that it would no longer be there whenever she wanted it. She burst into tears.

"Debbie, darling, whatever is it?"

"What's the matter, Princess?" Daddy asked.

"It's nice at Granny and Grandad's but I wanted to go on living with you," Debbie sobbed. "I'm glad you've got the baby if you wanted him but I really liked being your little girl and I wish it wasn't the new year!"

"Debbie." Mummy's eyes were watery again. "How could you think that we didn't want you?"

"You went all quiet when I was there. You were wondering what to do with me."

"Oh, Debs! We were worried for a little while because the baby seemed to be having a few problems." Mummy smiled. "But he's fine now. And of course you'll still be living with us — we both love you far too much ever to let you go. In fact, we were hoping that you would help us with him — babies are a lot of work."

"Come and say hello to your brother," her daddy said, lifting her off the bed.

Debbie studied the wrinkled, red face. She didn't think that she looked a bit like that, but she was far too happy to argue.

A tiny hand was protruding from the blanket and, as she touched it, the little fingers curled around hers and held on tightly. So he must have really wanted to meet her!

She smiled across to her parents and then down at her brother.

"Happy New Year, baby brother!" she whispered. ❏

Illustration by Majken Thorsen.

KATHIE always longed for a wet, really cold Bonfire Night, preferably with strong winds and snow. It wasn't that she was anti-fireworks, but November the fifth wasn't a good night for a Casualty nurse with a highly-strung cat.

Fireworks!

by Helen Owens

Now, seeing the man in front of her gleefully buying fireworks reminded her how close the hated day was. Realising he was her vet made it worse still.

"Hi, there." He turned to her and produced one of those killer grins that so often distracted her from Fluffy's injections. "Nice day."

"It is now, but you're going to make it a nightmare, aren't you?" she retorted. Part of her knew she was over-reacting at the end of a long day, but she just dreaded seeing the results of those fireworks arriving in her hospital, or hearing Fluffy's loud, terrified howl.

"Don't you think about what you're buying?"

"Pardon?" he asked.

His uncomprehending stare added fuel to the flames, and she went on fiercely.

"Fireworks are dangerous. I'd have thought you of all people would know that. If you don't, come to Casualty one evening this week and see what stupid kids do with them. If they're not throwing them at each other, they're burning themselves.

"Kids will be hurt this year, just like they always are, but you don't care, do you? Oh, no, you're going to have fun, and that's all that matters!"

155

"Actually —"

"No." Belatedly she realised everyone was staring and picked up her basket with all the dignity she could muster. "I'm not interested."

Cooling her heels in another, longer queue, she tried to work out why she'd reacted so fiercely. He *should* have known better, she thought, then wondered why she cared.

After all, he was just the man she took a loudly-complaining Persian to visit every month.

Just the man who made her knees go weak whenever he grinned at her. Just the best-looking thing in a white coat she'd ever seen, with a bedside manner that put most of the doctors she knew to shame.

The man who'd be expecting to see Fluffy next week . . .

"Oh, dear!" she muttered as she paid for her shopping, wondering how she'd get herself out of this one.

SHE thought about it during the few quiet moments on her shift the next day, but still hadn't come up with an answer when she saw him again, just as she was coming off duty.

She stopped dead. She'd known those blasted fireworks were trouble from the moment she'd seen them in his basket.

His hands were thrust in his pockets. Those beautiful, strong hands that Fluffy dug his claws into so often could be red and blistered because she hadn't stopped him buying those fireworks.

"Let's have a look." She summoned her most professional voice, wishing she hadn't changed out of her uniform.

"What?"

He must be in shock, she thought, clicking into professional mode. And that meant major burns and scarring and possibly long-term disability. She should have stopped him buying them somehow.

"Come and lie down."

"Hang on." Not only did he have that killer grin, but he had far too much charisma for one man when he laughed. "I'll have you know I'm not that sort of bloke!"

"Look." Her ministering angel mask slipped dramatically. "Are you hurt or not?"

"Not. I thought I'd take you up on your invitation. You know," he explained helpfully when she didn't say anything, "the one you yelled in front of the whole shop? About me seeing what my toys were capable of?"

"Oh." She looked at her sensible shoes, then gritted her teeth. "I'm sorry. I shouldn't have said all that."

"I was a bit surprised," he agreed, then shuffled his feet. "I don't suppose it'd do any good if I said that I agree with you, and I'm doing the fireworks for the school."

"The school?" On the plus side he wasn't an arrogant, non-safety-conscious fool. On the minus side, being involved with a school usually meant kids.

And kids meant wives. So that was another dream out of the window.

"That's right. It's a place where kids go to learn stuff. My kids."

"I know what a school is!" She snorted, then looked round the unusually empty Casualty unit. She'd have liked to show him something really hideous — something that would explain why she'd felt so passionate, and so drained.

She hated seeing anyone hurt, but children were the worst. They didn't understand that they could be hurt. As for the expressions on the parents' faces . . .

"Rough day?" he asked sympathetically, and she realised that he didn't need to see a burns victim to understand.

"Rough week," she affirmed. "And I hate fireworks. Fluffy gets in such a state."

"That cat gets in a state about everything," he pointed out with a grin.

"It's not his fault! My gran spoiled him. I really am sorry."

"Don't look so worried, Kathie."

"How do you know my name?"

"It's on your appointment card. I see it each time, and —" he smiled shyly "— I always think it suits you."

"Thanks," she muttered. He had the advantage over her. She knew him as Mr J. Stevens and she'd often wondered what the "J" stood for.

"Jason," he said suddenly, then laughed when she jumped. "And I'm not psychic. Anyway, I know you're tired so I won't keep you, but I wondered if you'd like to come along to the firework display.

"Before you ask, I'm divorced and the kids live with their mum, but I love them dearly and if I don't bring someone to the fireworks they'll spend all evening matchmaking for me."

As first dates went, it had to be the least romantic invitation ever, but at least it was an invite. And she had to refuse it . . .

"It's not that I don't want to come, but —" She paused, knowing it sounded stupid. "I'm scared of fireworks, and someone should stay with Fluffy and —"

"How can I bear coming second place to the cat?" When he turned and smiled at her, she knew her crush could easily turn into something more.

Together, they walked to her car.

"Well?" he asked as she unlocked the door. "I'll understand if you don't want to come."

"I've got to get over it some time." As ways of saying "yes" went, it was about as romantic as his invitation, but he seemed to understand.

She'd never felt excited about Bonfire Night before, which made it all the more unfair that November the fifth was wet. Quite exceptionally wet, in fact. The sort of driving rain that causes traffic accidents, makes little old ladies slip on pavements and break bones and causes havoc with people's bronchitis and arthritis.

With all that happening, it wasn't surprising that Kathie couldn't get off duty on time. She tried ringing the surgery, but all she got was an answering machine.

"It's not fair," she muttered as she eventually drove home. She'd started to like the idea of a cold, crisp Bonfire Night. He'd hold her hand to stop her feeling scared and she would see his face lit by firelight and they'd talk and laugh together . . .

She parked the car, squelched up the path, then felt a hand on her arm and yelped.

"Hey!" Jason said, and she sagged against him in pure, tired relief.

"What's up?" He sounded like he did when he examined Fluffy. Very quiet, very gentle and very concerned. She knew she was safe with him.

"Nothing, but I wasn't expecting you to be here," she admitted.

"We had a date, didn't we?"

"An hour ago. Most men leave."

"Most men aren't vets. I know what it's like," he said simply.

"Bad day?" he asked as they went inside.

"Awful." She took off her flat shoes and wriggled her aching feet. "Just give me ten minutes to change."

"Kathie, Kathie." She'd never realised how beautiful his voice was before. "Any display tonight would be a real damp squib. It's tomorrow instead, but —" He ran his hand through his wet hair, then smiled and she knew whatever else might be a damp squib, the feelings between them definitely weren't.

"I'm here, you're too tired to cook, or do anything else. How about a take-away and a night with the TV?"

It mightn't be romantic, but it sounded as wonderful as it turned out to be, and memories of that great evening kept her going while she waited for his surgery to finish the following night.

It ran so late that they almost missed the display altogether, but it didn't matter. The spark between them was definitely growing into a bright flame. ❏

Durham

LIKE many towns in the North of England, Durham is rich in beautiful buildings and ancient stories. The magnificent 11th century cathedral itself is a fine example of this. According to a legend on one of the cathedral's turrets, the cathedral owes its existence to a milkmaid who led wandering monks to their final home.

On the cliffs above the River Wear — which frames the town almost on all sides — Durham Castle was built in 1832 to replace the existing ruins. It holds the illustrious honour of being the only northern fortress never to fall to the marauding Scots — an impressive feat, indeed!

DURHAM: J CAMPBELL KERR

by Jill Hyem

THERE was pandemonium in the toy department. Lavinia Partridge, on her way to the staff cafeteria for her coffee break, stopped in her tracks. This was not just the usual seasonal hubbub. Something was seriously amiss.

Small children were wailing, women's voices were raised in angry protest, inexperienced shop assistants, newly recruited for the Christmas rush, were running about like demented ants. The source of the uproar seemed to emanate from the far end, beyond Fluffy Toys, where Father Christmas's Fairy Grotto was temporarily housed.

"Oh, Miss Partridge, thank goodness!" One of the young assistants hurried towards Lavinia, recognising her as the person who had interviewed her for the job.

"What on earth's going on?"

"It's Father Christmas!" the girl panted. "He's locked himself in the Grotto and refuses to come out."

"Why? Is he ill?" Lavinia asked anxiously. She had noticed that Hector Antrobus, the elderly actor who had been Father Christmas for the past five years, had not seemed quite his jolly self this time.

"No, I don't think he's sick. He just — sort of blew his top."

Before Lavinia could question the girl further, a slow handclap started in the background and a chorus of voices began to chant "Why are we waiting?"

All I Want Fo

Steeling herself for action, Lavinia made her way to the entrance to the Grotto, where the disgruntled crowd was gathered. Some of the children were ransacking the discarded sack of toys, while others were throwing polystyrene snowballs at each other.

Cowering against the wall behind them, her wings flattened, was Fairy Snow — alias Tracey Alsop, whom Lavinia herself had plucked from the safe anonymity of Kitchenware to be Father Christmas's helper. She looked close to tears.

Lavinia quickly positioned herself on the rostrum, trying to remember all the things she had learned on her recent self-assertion course. She took a deep breath.

"Excuse me, ladies," she called, raising her hand for silence. "And gentlemen," she added hastily, noticing a few embarrassed-looking fathers amongst the rabble. "May we please have a little hush?"

160

Christmas...

Illustration by Nygård.

    Recognising the voice of authority the mob turned towards her. The noise gradually subsided until the tinny recording of "Jingle Bells" could be heard again.

    "Thank you." Lavinia smiled placatingly. "I am Lavinia Partridge, Deputy Head of Human Resources."

    "What are they when they're at home?" someone shouted. Lavinia explained, as she was inevitably obliged to do. (Whyever did they change it from Personnel?)

    "Now," she continued, "let's see if we can sort things out."

    "You'd better," a cross-looking woman muttered. "We paid for our tickets, and what do we get? Shoddy toys, and verbal abuse from Santa-flippin'-Claus who then pushes off into his cave without so much as a pardon me. Bad-tempered old buffer."

    Mustering all her managerial skills, Lavinia swiftly took matters in hand.

161

"Allow me to apologise on behalf of Oliver's for any inconvenience you have been caused," she said. "I am afraid Father Christmas is currently indisposed." She ignored the derisive jeers.

"Naturally, your ticket money will be refunded at once. Unless, that is, you would prefer to wait for a while in the Rainbow Restaurant, where free coffee will be served. And, of course, fruit juice for the children. Someone will call you as soon as Father Christmas is back."

She then dispatched one of the assistants to see the restaurant manager and another to deal with the refunds. As the crowd started to disperse she turned to the snivelling Fairy Snow.

"Now pull yourself together, Tracey. Take a break, wash your face, adjust your wings and be back in ten minutes."

"But what about Father Christmas?" the girl stammered.

"Leave him to me," Lavinia said grimly, as she pinned up the notice that read *Gone to feed the reindeer. Back soon.*

WHAT Lavinia hated more than anything was a lack of professionalism, something that was only too common, alas, in this day and age. If you undertook to do a job, you did it properly. She herself had only been off work once during her entire career at Oliver's, and that was when her mother had had a stroke in the middle of the Summer Sales.

Besides, Hector Antrobus was an actor. Surely he, of all people, should know that the show must go on no matter what? Yet he had always been so reliable in the past, and popular with the children and parents.

He was the ideal Father Christmas, with his rosy cheeks and smiling blue eyes. That was why she had selected him from the ten candidates who had applied for the job five Christmases ago.

She didn't know him well, but each year when he returned they exchanged a few friendly words. He had struck her as a likeable, solid person. Perhaps after all, she reflected, he was not feeling well.

Bracing herself, Lavinia knocked on the door of the Grotto, a large garden shed that had been converted for the occasion.

"Mr Antrobus?" she called.

There was no reply.

"Mr Antrobus, this is Miss Partridge from Personnel — er — Human Resources. Will you please open the door?"

There was another pause. Lavinia was about to summon one of the men from DIY to break the lock when she heard the key turning slowly.

"You'd best come in," said a gruff voice that sounded very different from the actor's usual jocular tone.

She opened the door and stepped inside.

For a moment, she couldn't see too clearly. The Grotto was lit only by twinkling fairy lights and magic lanterns, which contrasted with the bright strip lighting in the store outside.

As her eyes grew accustomed to the rosy glow she discerned a figure sitting hunched on the yule log in the corner, his head in his hands. He looked up as she approached.

She noticed that he had taken off the long white beard. It lay abandoned on the floor nearby.

"GO on then," he said wretchedly. "Fire me. I know I deserve it. All these years as Father Christmas and I let one spoiled brat put an end to my days at Oliver's. Some of the happiest days of my life." He sighed melodramatically.

"May we have less of the histrionics?" Lavinia said crisply.

"Give me my cards straight away, then, and I'll hang up my hood and depart."

"I am not here to sack you, Mr Antrobus. I am hoping that will not be necessary. I simply wish to ascertain what caused you to desert your post."

He looked at her and she saw that the blue eyes were rimmed with red, and that there were dark circles beneath them that spoke of sleepless nights. She drew up a toadstool and sat down beside him.

"I am sure you would not have acted as you did without considerable provocation. I know what modern children can be like."

"It's not their fault. It's the way of the world these days. The magic's gone out of Christmas. They've got too much, that's the trouble. All they want are computer games and mobile phones and personal stereos. When I think of the little things that used to please me as a lad . . . Oh, the joy of a plastic whistle or a chocolate sovereign."

"And a tangerine in the toe of your stocking," Lavinia murmured, looking back nostalgically to her own spartan childhood.

"And if Father Christmas asked me, 'Do you eat up your cabbage like a good boy?' I most certainly did not tell him to get —" He broke off. "I won't repeat his language in front of you, Miss Partridge. But the mother was every bit as bad."

"Nevertheless, Mr Antrobus, you must have come across equally troublesome children before," Lavinia said, pursing her lips.

"You're right," he admitted dolefully. "And after all, I'm a *pro*. I've dealt with hostile audiences from Harwich to Hartlepool and come out unscathed. And you don't do panto for twenty years without learning how to handle difficult kiddies. Reg and I used to pride ourselves on our rapport with the youngsters."

"Reg?"

He looked subdued again.

"A friend of mine. We used to do a double act together in the old days. Ugly Sisters, Brokers' Men, Bos'un and Mate. You know the sort of thing."

She did indeed. She and her mother had never missed going to the pantomime. It was the highlight of the festive season.

"But in latter years," Hector continued, "the panto engagements tailed off. They only wanted soap stars and sports celebrities. And then Oliver's came to my rescue, thanks to your good self. You don't know what it meant to me, Miss Partridge. But for you it would have been my first Christmas unemployed. Reg managed to to get a job as Chief Weasel in 'Toad of Toad Hall', but I had no prospect of anything."

Lavinia had never liked to ask Hector about his work. It might have been tactless, for actors, as she knew, spent a great deal of time "resting", as they called it.

She looked at her watch and remembered the marauding mothers and children waiting in the Rainbow Restaurant.

"Getting back to the current situation . . ." she prompted.

"Oh — yes. The fact is, Miss Partridge, it suddenly got to me. All those kids saying 'I want', when half the world is starving. And then when that child gave me lip . . . I was almost tempted to hit him."

"Thank heavens you didn't do that." Lavinia had sudden visions of Oliver's being sued by the parents and headlines all over the tabloids: *Father Christmas Assaults Eight Year Old*.

"I just don't know what got into me. I wouldn't have let you down for the world."

She noticed that without the beard he looked younger. He couldn't be that much

White Wilderness

THE snowbound forest deep
Lies wrapped in silence under Arctic skies
The hills are all asleep.
No golden eagle flies,
Nor fluting note is heard
From moorland bird —
Even the fox has sought her lonely lair!
No breath of wind disturbs the frosty air,
Nor lilting stream
Wakens the woodland from its wintry dream
Yet, in this frozen land,
The hungry deer come tamely to the hand,
And sleepless pine trees stand
Watchful amid the silent wilderness
As if they know
That, in a while the sunlight will return
To warm the hills, and every melting burn.
Then a joyous song will sing,
While all the woods awake to loveliness,
And snowdrops nod their bonnets in the snow
To welcome radiant spring!

— *Brenda G. Macro*

Highland stag in winter forest, Laggan.

older than she was.

"Perhaps you were feeling a bit under the weather?" she suggested.

"I must admit I haven't been quite myself lately."

"Have you seen a doctor?"

"There's nothing a doctor can do. It's more a state of mind. It's just . . . my friend Reg passed away a month ago."

"I'm so sorry. Would you like to talk about it?" she asked tentatively.

For a moment he said nothing. Then he nodded.

"I'd known him since we were lads, over forty years. We did a summer season in Llandudno, and we clicked at once. Same interests, same sense of humour. We kept up afterwards, but then our lives went along different paths for a time.

"We both got married, and then divorced. It's not easy in our business to provide the sort of stable life a young woman wants."

"Did you have any children?"

165

"No. I would have liked them, mind. I suppose panto and Father Christmas was the next best thing. Anyway, Reg and I met up again in 'Dick Whittington' and, to cut a long story short, we ended up sharing a flat in Herne Hill.

"Not that we were both there all the time. Like as not, one of us was away on tour or doing a stint in repertory. But the flat was our base, our roots. And special times — like Christmas — we always spent together. As I say, we did panto every year, but Christmas Day we had off.

"Reg used to cook the meal. He'd once done a cookery course between jobs . . . Then afterwards, we'd have a Port and watch old films on the telly and maybe play chess. We were what you'd call — in the words of Mr Priestley — good companions."

His face clouded over again.

"The flat seems so empty now. And the thought of spending Christmas on my own . . ." He tailed off, then, forcing a smile, went on. "You must think I'm a right old misery."

"No, actually, I don't." She knew exactly how he felt. The last two Christmases since her mother had passed on had been lonely times for her, too.

She had volunteered to help with the Old People's Christmas Lunch, and had thrown herself into it all, pulling crackers and joining in the sing-songs. But at the end of the day she had had to go back to the empty house which seemed so much emptier at Christmas.

"Still," Hector said, perking up a bit, "I've got my memories. I shall look through all our photographs and press cuttings, and relive those happy shows. 'Cinderella' at Watford, 'Robinson Crusoe' at Grimsby, 'Aladdin' at Weston-super-Mare . . ."

"Weston-super-Mare?"

"Yes. That was the last panto Reg and I did together. Six years ago. I was Widow Twankey."

"But I must have *seen* you!" Lavinia exclaimed.

"You never!"

"I did. Mother and I spent Christmas there that year, and we went to the pantomime on Boxing Day."

"'Aladdin'?"

"Yes, and it was wonderful. One of the best we'd ever seen."

"Really?" His face lit up.

"Yes, we both said so. And you were Widow Twankey, just imagine! Of course, I didn't recognise you when you came to the interview at Oliver's."

"Well, you wouldn't, would you, not without my sausage curls and my red bloomers." They both chuckled, then sat for a moment in silence, sharing the delight of the memory. Then Lavinia looked at her watch again.

"Oh, dear, look at the time. I think Father Christmas has been feeding his reindeer for quite long enough. Do you feel up to facing the fray again, Mr Antrobus? They're waiting for you in the restaurant."

He hesitated, then picked up the abandoned beard.

"Then we mustn't keep them, must we? On with the show!" he said with his old bravado.

"I'll go and summon them," Lavinia said thankfully.

"One minute, Miss Partridge . . ."

She stopped.

"Yes?"

"I just wanted to say thank you. You're a real pal."

Lavinia felt a sudden surge of emotion. As she reached the door she turned back.

"I wonder . . ." she said. "Would you care to come round for a drink and a mince-pie on Christmas Night?"

He looked at her with disbelief.

"I shall be on my own, too," she added. "You'd be very welcome."

"There's nothing I'd like better." He smiled delightedly.

"And perhaps you could bring some of your pantomime photographs with you. I should love to see them."

Lavinia came out of the Fairy Grotto and took down the notice. As she headed for the restaurant there was a new spring in her step. This year, Christmas wouldn't be so empty after all. ❑

MARNI lived for the sound of the waves crashing in from the Atlantic, fracturing in huge billows of white against the rocks. At this time of year, with the summer dying and dwindling, the few hardy holidaymakers who remained in town huddled against the wind, their clothes flapping and blustering, their faces set against the cold.

Soon, the beach would be empty, belonging only to herself and Thrasher, her dog, another of her good causes. Abandoned by his previous owner, he was small of body, large and active of tail — hence the name.

He was wagging it now, ferociously, as reluctant as Marni to leave the beach. But work awaited. She pointed herself firmly in the direction of the Aqua-arium, Thrasher trailing grudgingly behind her.

"Can you save it, miss?"

A small boy with a large bucket was waiting impatiently outside the large double entrance doors. Marni put the bucket down on the floor and stirred its murky depths with one finger.

Thrasher whined, and the man accompanying the little boy bent down and patted the dog soothingly. Inside the bucket, something pale and bloated stirred fretfully.

"Ah . . . Hippocarpus . . ." She saw the puzzlement on his face and smiled up at him.

"The common seahorse," she explained. "They're always getting washed up on the shore. I'll see what I can do."

The children always brought their finds to the Aqua-arium, demanding miracles. Bernie, Marni thought, amused, would be furious.

"Harry . . . his name's Harry." The little boy's face was rather pinched.

"He's a dragon . . ."

His companion raised his eyes apologetically. They were nice eyes, brown and gentle. Marni realised she had seen him up at the holiday camp, with the party of inner-city children who were on a trip subsidised by end-of-season rates and money from the local council.

"Go and get yourself an ice-cream and then wait by the van." The man pulled a coin from his pocket and dropped it into the boy's grubby hand.

They watched him run across the road and over to the tea-bar by the steps leading down to the beach.

Illustration by
Heidi Spindler.

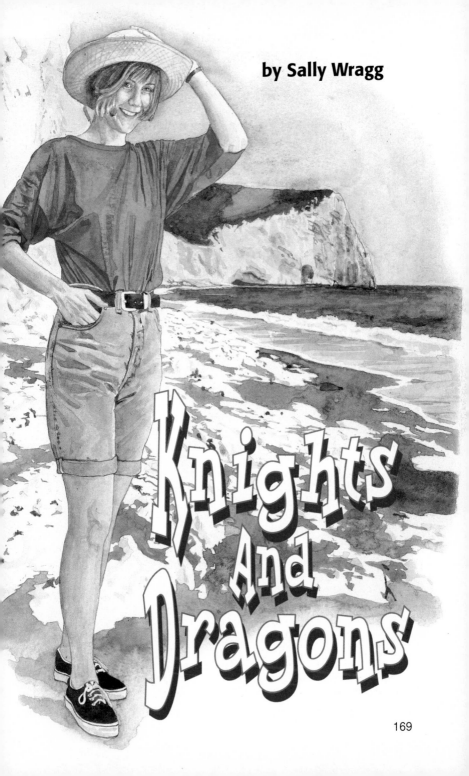

by **Sally Wragg**

Knights And Dragons

"I'm Derek . . ."

"Marni . . ."

"It's good of you to take the trouble," he began.

"I can't promise anything . . ."

"No, of course not. Perhaps it would have been kinder just to return it to the rock pool where we found it? Let nature take its course?"

"No, really. I'll see what I can do. Call back tomorrow."

She watched him go and then unlocked the doors to the Aqua-arium and went inside, carrying the bucket carefully. Thrasher's claws pattered after her on the wooden floorboards. Where Marni went, Thrasher followed.

Carefully, she tilted the water into an empty aquarium and watched the seahorse slide into it and down to the bottom of the tank where it undulated slowly like a small, pale ghost.

She didn't hold out much hope.

"MARNI." Bernie, her boss, bustled in, his bald head glistening greenly under the aquarium lights.

"What have you got now?" he demanded, sounding cross, as usual.

"It's a seahorse," she explained hastily, waiting for the explosion. "Someone brought it in not five minutes since."

"What do you think this is — underwater Animal Hospital? This isn't a charity! Sometimes I don't think you realise . . ." He continued in this vein for some time before going into his office and slamming the door.

Marni waited. Sure enough, moments later, the door re-opened and Bernie's head appeared.

"You'd better raise the temperature in the tank to give the poor little blighter a chance . . ." The head disappeared abruptly.

Poor, dear Bernie! You only had to hang around long enough and the real one always emerged, despite all his best intentions. Marni laughed out loud.

She was busy all day, cleaning the tanks, feeding the fish, taking the occasional entrance money, being on hand to answer queries and man the phones.

Now and then she checked on her patient. There didn't seem to be any improvement.

In the evening, she took Thrasher for a bracing walk along the beach, stopping now and then to pick up a sea-shell for her collection, rubbing its shiny smoothness against her jacket before dropping it into a small cloth bag she carried for the purpose.

The wind whipped her hair across her face, snatching at her breath in gasps. She could taste the sea on her lips and the sun, sinking down on the horizon, cast an orange glow against the green-grey waters, flecked with froths of greeny-white.

"It's wonderful isn't it? I love the sound of the sea."

Derek appeared by her side. He made the mistake of bending down, allowing Thrasher the opportunity of treating his face to an all-over wash.

"Er . . . A bit enthusiastic, isn't he?" He grimaced and then laughed.

"He's nearly as bad as my parents' dog."

Marni laughed and pulled Thrasher away.

"Are you on your own?" She was used to seeing him surrounded by crowds of schoolchildren, looking exhausted.

"I do get time off occasionally — and you could say I need it!"

"I bet."

He picked up a shell from the shingle and handed it to her.

"Here . . . I saw you collecting these earlier."

It was smooth and pale pink with fluted edges. She closed her hand around it, wondering how long he had been watching her.

"I was just on my way for a drink," he explained. "Would you . . . care to join me?"

She almost found herself agreeing before she reluctantly remembered she had decided against any more entanglements. No more allowing her feelings to become engaged in what were, after all, no more than holiday romances, on their side at least.

The men in her life were always running back home before she had the chance to get to know them properly, promising to write, keep in touch, even get over to see her again some time . . .

If she was lucky, she occasionally received the odd postcard or two before she became a pleasant blur in their collective memories. She had become a perpetual pleasant interlude before real life intervened. She had decided it simply wasn't worth it.

The sea was coming in now on waves like white horses.

"Sorry, I have to get Thrasher home for his dinner."

"What a shame. We're going back home the day after tomorrow, the new term's starting."

She left him reluctantly, Thrasher panting at her side.

At work the following morning, she went straight to the seahorse's tank, still wondering if she had been wrong not to have a drink with Derek. What harm could it have done? But then, she thought, what would have been the point if he was going home tomorrow? Why start something you couldn't finish?

She hardly dared to look at her patient.

What she discovered in the tank made her gasp in astonishment.

IT wasn't until her coffee break that Derek and the boy finally arrived. They stood at the door, Derek's hand on the boy's shoulders, his eyes warm with an appreciation she could hardly mistake. Despite her best intentions, Marni's heart skipped a beat.

"How's Harry?" the boy demanded at once.

"Over here." Marni couldn't keep the laughter from her voice. She took him over to the tank.

"Things have . . . escalated a little during the night!"

An explosion of sea-horses undulated backwards and forwards like tiny mermen, Harry in the middle of the densest throng of them, dorsal fin quivering in a proud paternal ownership.

"Well, I'll be blowed!" Derek's eyes were alive with laughter. "I bet you never expected this, Robbie."

But Robbie's bottom lip was thrust forward in obvious disappointment.

"What's the matter?" She had thought he would be pleased.

"Well — he's not a Harry, is he?" Robbie burst out, as if it were obvious. His eyes were suspiciously bright, and he rubbed at them furiously.

"He's a she!"

Couldn't dragons be girls?

Hastily, Marni began to explain.

"Seahorses are very unusual creatures, Robbie. The lady seahorse lays her eggs in the pouch the male has in the front here and he incubates them until they grow into miniature seahorses, just like these. No wonder Harry looked so fat and lazy; he was only waiting for this lot to pop out!"

"Wow!" Robbie's face brightened at once.

"I'll release them all back into the sea shortly," she said, pleased at least someone would be going home happy.

"Thanks, miss. All those dragons . . ." He placed one grubby hand against the glass. "Bye, Harry," he whispered. "I can't wait to tell me mates . . . Come on, sir!"

He was off, nearly out of the door already, his mind clambering over rocks, discovering fresh pools, new adventures with dragons.

"Thanks, Marni, it's been really good of you to take the trouble. I'm only sorry . . ." Derek's voice trailed away, as if he wanted to say more and didn't quite know how.

"I'd better go after him." He sighed gently, and then he was gone, before Marni had the chance to say goodbye.

Derek and his party of children were leaving tomorrow. What if, this time, things were different and Derek was the one who would really have kept in touch? She rather thought now he might. She should have trusted her instincts and given things a chance.

It was too late now.

A FEW lonely weeks later, Harry and his brood were ready to return to their natural home. Marni decided to wait until the early evening, until she had the place all to herself.

Having made such a fuss at their unplanned arrival, Bernie had now decided the seahorses would be an added attraction for the following season and he wanted to keep them.

But they had come out of the ocean, and they were going back there. It was the right thing to do, Marni knew. His wrath would soon blow itself out in any case.

Marni only wished she could dismiss her feelings towards Derek as easily. It was ridiculous, but she couldn't get him out of her mind. Why hadn't she asked for his address whilst she had the chance? And why exactly couldn't she forget him?

She carried her cargo carefully over to the largest rock pool in a large white plastic sandwich box. The tide was already coming in. A crab scuttled hastily over a rock and disappeared.

The sea-breeze fanned her face, the setting sun a pale disc on the horizon, trailing a widening slant of pale pink over the shifting waters.

Thrasher seemed to have found himself a companion at any rate, a mongrel of seemingly similar parentage. The two dogs perched themselves by the edge of the rocks to watch the proceedings, tails thumping in unison.

"Ah . . . I thought I'd find you here," a familiar voice said.

"Derek!" Marni sprang up at once, her face flushing like the setting sun. It was as if her thoughts had taken pity on her misery and brought themselves to life.

"But what . . ."

"Am I doing here?" He finished the question. "Taking the dog for a walk!"

He smiled towards Thrasher's new-found companion.

"He belongs to my parents, actually. They live just up past the holiday camp. Didn't I tell you? They retired here this spring."

"No, you didn't." She frowned momentarily. "I don't suppose I ever gave you the chance."

"We could soon rectify that." Derek's eyes twinkled good-humouredly. "It's not as if I don't visit them a lot — I'm always over here."

Marni could hear her own heartbeat pounding in her ears. Or was it only the echo of the waves, crashing with relentless futility against the shore?

Quietly, she went down and slid the contents of the container into the pool. She watched as the little creatures swam away. All those dragons . . .

Marni looked up and smiled. Well, with all those dragons to contend with, it stood to reason there would be a handsome knight around somewhere . . . ❏

Printed and Published in Great Britain by D.C. Thomson & Co., Ltd., Dundee, Glasgow and London.
© D.C. Thomson & Co., 2002. While every reasonable care will be taken,
neither D.C. Thomson., Ltd., nor its agents will accept liability for loss or damage to colour
transparencies or any other material submitted to this publication.

ISBN 0-85116-818-3
EAN 9-780851-168180

London

SEEN from the great height of the London Eye, the country's capital is a breathtaking sight. All along the curving River Thames are examples of this fine city's history and importance.

The Houses of Parliament sit majestically on one side while, further down on the opposite bank, the beautifully recreated Globe theatre and the thought-provoking Tate Modern are just a tube ride away.